Harvest of a Wrathful Eye
An Outer Banks Crime Mystery

Colin Beckett

Colin Beckett

Harvest of a Wrathful Eye
An Outer Banks Crime Mystery

Once again, for Charlene.
With love and gratitude, and for the many memories
that are made every day.

"In common things that round us lie
Some random things he can impart, -
The harvest of a quiet eye,
That broods and sleeps on his own heart."

William Wordsworth
1770 – 1850

"Those who live only to satisfy
their own sinful nature
will harvest decay and death
from that sinful nature."

Galatians 6:8

Harvest of a Wrathful Eye

Prologue

The Strawberry Moon shone bright in the heavens above the tranquil waters of The Lost Colony Cove Marina nestled in the harbor of the Roanoke Sound. The sport fishermen had long since called it a day. Just a sprinkling of boat and luxury yacht owners were cleaning up their vessels making them ready for a run the next morning. Others were enjoying cocktails with invited friends aboard their moored and gently bobbing watercraft at the end of a picture-perfect weather day in June along North Carolina's Outer Banks.

The intruder swam only a small distance, and making use of the ladder that was supplied to board or disembark boats, he climbed aboard an empty docking slip, pulled the snorkel from his mouth, and slid his mask over the hood of his Neoprene wetsuit. He walked a few paces wearing his fins to a wooden bench situated in some shadow cover, seated himself to get his bearings, and began to surveil his unsuspecting mark covertly from this safe distance.

Despite his family's wealth, he didn't own a membership to this exclusive club. Besides, he had heard his mother say that a boat is just a hole in the water that you pour money into. Had he chosen to drive, it would have been difficult to gain admission at the front gate. There would have been too many questions from the nosy security dicks about why he wanted to gain entrance at night, and his movements closely watched by elaborate surveillance cameras. Snorkeling into the marina from the Washington Baum Bridge boat ramp was the best play. It was as if he had cast a real-life role for himself based upon one of his favorite Tom Cruise *Mission Impossible* movies. Here he was. He made it. It was a stealthy, premeditated and deadly job that he was undertaking. The odds of success overwhelmingly against him. And he was finding it to be totally delicious.

From the waterproof hip sack worn around his waist he withdrew a pair of small yet powerful Bushnell binoculars so that he could better scan his target as well as the adjoining watercraft across from him. His mark was sitting in a chair drinking what looked like a bottle of beer at the stern of his impressive yacht.

This was problematic. The intruder needed him to be in the cabin below deck if he was going to keep the element of surprise in his favor. Still, the other boats in the adjoining slips were dark and devoid of any human activity. So far, so good.

For nearly a quarter of an hour, little happened, when he suddenly observed his mark taking a pull from the long neck bottle, turning it upside down over the boat's railing, and emptied the last few drops into the marina. Then he stood up and stretched and disappeared quickly below deck into the cabin. Through a porthole, the intruder could see that a light had been turned on. It was time to make his play. He put the binoculars back in his hip sack, slipped his mask over his face and walked back towards the ladder. He dropped into the water and in no time at all he was alongside his target vessel. He climbed the ladder on to the dock where he slid the fins off of his feet, took off his mask and snorkel, and silently boarded the boat.

Once on board, he scanned his surroundings. He was in his mid-twenties and stood exactly six feet tall. The black hooded wetsuit enhanced the lithe, athletic muscles of his biceps and thighs. All was still quiet. He took out a pair of vinyl gloves from his hip sack and put them on. Next, he withdrew a .22 – cal. Browning Buckmark and screwed an eight-inch suppressor into the end of its threaded barrel. It looked like a weapon used in all the classic mafia hit man movies. He held the gun with his right hand along the length of his right leg, and leading with his left he began to creep down the steps of the narrow passageway that led to the cabin. The unmistakable odor of microwave popcorn wafted up into his nostrils. He hated popcorn.

"Who the fuck are you and what are you doing on my boat?" The mark demanded as he sat bolt upright in a captain's chair with a bowl of popcorn and a brown long neck beer bottle on a small table beside him. A magazine was open on his lap. The intruder knew that the mark was in his forties, and out of shape. His paunch suggested that he enjoyed food and drink more than regular exercise. *I wonder what she saw in _him_ besides a lot of money*, the intruder thought briefly to himself before he returned to the matter at hand.

"I'm Death," the intruder said as he brought the weapon out from around his hip and pointed it at the mark. "I'm death on two legs."

"Look buddy, I've done nothing to you. Put the gun away. Let's talk."

He put out both his hands, palms out facing the floor, and slowly waved them up and down in a calming gesture.

"There's nothing to talk about, Phil. I'm not one of your crazy psych patients that you're shrink wrapping. I know exactly what I'm doing, so shut the fuck up," the hooded intruder said.

"How do you know my name and what it is that I do?"

There was no reply from the intruder. The gun was still leveled at his eyes. Seconds seemed to pass like agonizing minutes.

"Look... I've got a safe right over there," the victim said as he hiked his head towards the opposite side of the cabin. "I've got a lot of cash inside. It's yours. Just put the gun away, and take it and leave me be, O.K.?"

The intruder smiled.

"You probably keep a gun in that safe too, huh?"

"No! No gun. Just cash and a passport. Look, you've got the drop on me. Let me open the safe and get the cash and you can split? I won't tell the cops about any of this. Okay?"

"Okay. Open the safe. But remember that I'm younger and stronger than and twice as fast as you. If you're lying about a gun, you'll be dead where you stand."

"Okay. Just take it easy," Phil said as he slowly got up and walked the short distance across the cabin to a small wooden wall panel that he opened which revealed a small metal safe. He put his right hand on the combination wheel and with a few rotations a small click could be heard.

"Step back and sit down in your chair," the intruder said. "I'll take it from here."

"Sure. No problem." He did as instructed while the intruder removed a sizable stack of fresh $50 bills from the safe and stuffed it into his hip sack.

"Now it will look like a robbery," the intruder said as he pointed the weapon back at his helpless victim. "Committed by one of your barmy patients who went 'round the bend and *snapped*." He snapped his gloved left thumb and forefinger for effect. Dr. Phillip McCleney's hands were shaking as he held them out defensively and crossed them in front of his face, as if skin and sinew and bone could block a steel bullet traveling at 1200 feet per second. He looked at the end of the gun barrel then back up at the face of the hooded intruder.

"Look, I don't understand. You've got my money. You seem to know some things about me. I've got nothing to lose by asking... What's this all about, for crissake?"

The intruder cocked his head back and cackled out loud.

"Okay. What this is all about is that I'm here to kill *you* because I don't kill women. And because... Well because... She said, 'No.'"

"Who is 'she'?"

"Anne, of course."

The intruder quickly straightened his arm and took a bead down the long barrel of the weapon and fired a bullet into Dr. Phillip McCleney's forehead. All that was heard inside the cabin was the lightning fast racking of the cold metal slide and the ping of the small bullet cartridge glancing off a metallic surface in the cabin. Suddenly, the odor of gunpowder trumped the stale smell of popcorn.

The intruder disassembled the weapon and put the two pieces back into his hip sack. He didn't need to police his brass since he had taken the precaution of wearing gloves when he loaded the magazine. He then withdrew a pair of sharp pruning shears from the sack. He took up the shears and strode over to the cadaver slumped in his chair, and harvested the wedding ring finger from the dead man's left hand.

"Bloody hell," the intruder said in the empty space as he placed the severed digit in a small, plastic, fold- top sandwich bag and shoved it into his hip sack.

He zipped up the sack while he stared at his butchery and contemplated his next move. He looked down at his $1200 diver's watch and noted that only thirty minutes had passed since he first boarded the boat. The only remorse that he felt was for himself, because he wouldn't be able to see Anne's face when she received the news about poor 'ol Phil.

"*Bitch*," he said angrily to the moonlit sky.

Once he was back topside on the dock, he retrieved the dismembered finger from the hip sack and threw it into the Roanoke Sound. He put his fins back on his feet, pulled the diver's mask over his face, grabbed his snorkel, and dropped like a stone into the calm dark water, and slithered like a python back to the boat ramp where his expensive car was parked.

One Month Ago

The Stony Man Overlook along mile 41.7 of the Skyline Drive inside the Shenandoah National Park was closed off in both directions by the Virginia State Police cars sent from Division Two headquarters in Culpeper. A peregrine falcon circled overhead briefly intrigued by all of the busy human activity at the base of the mountain, where personnel from the Scientific Investigation Division were examining and photographing human remains.

Lt. Jared McClure of the State Police Area 14 Office in Luray had been dispatched to the scene. Following hours of lowering equipment – descending the highest point along the Skyline Drive – he and Trooper Fred Drury were now getting the first reports and tentative hypotheses from the SID people.

"So, how long has our dead body been a part of the park's flora and fauna," McClure said as he wiped away the free-flowing sweat off of his forehead with a white handkerchief. It was a warm, overcast day in May.

"Our best educated guess is that it has been here for about a year given the state of decomposition. It's the remains of a male victim - age to be determined - who was discovered by a couple of hikers early this morning," the SID tech said. She was in her late twenties; petite and blond and blue-eyed, and she showed no visible signs of exertion due to climbing over large boulders in the high humidity. "Mulcahey" was the name stenciled on her name plate.

McClure on the other hand was a 6' 4" giant of a guy in his late thirties, with male pattern baldness on the crown of his thinning crop of brown hair, which seemed to match the color of his eyes. He and Drury were each wearing the standard summer uniform consisting of light gray button-up short-sleeved shirts, gray pants with a dark blue stripe down the sides, black shoes and black semi-gloss straw campaign hats, also known as "Smokey the Bear" wear.

"Any clue as to cause of death?"
He looked up towards the Overlook, clouds temporarily blocking the sun which afforded him a better look.

"Yes. That we know. Shot in the forehead by a small caliber round."

Unfazed, McClure nodded and looked over at Trooper Drury, who like Mulcahey, was in his mid-twenties. He was fresh out of the Academy, and stood 5' 10" tall with black hair and green eyes. He was taking notes on a small, spiral bound pad of white paper.

"Anything else you can make out given the condition of the remains?" McClure said.

"Yes sir," Mulcahey said. "His wedding ring finger is missing."

Drury looked up from his notepad. "Probably gnawed off by critters," he said.

"Negative, Trooper," she said. "Even after a year out here in these elements I can tell that it was an amputation. It was done by some sort of sharp instrument. I don't know if the victim had been tortured, or if the amputation was postmortem. I'll know more when we get him on the table, of course."

"Do you think that he was shot and killed here?" McClure said as he scanned the surroundings dotted with Virginia and Eastern white pine trees.

"That's very hard to say right now but my gut tells me that it's unlikely. Judging by the position and location of the remains, and the tattered clothing, I'd say the deceased was most likely thrown out of a trunk of a car from up there." Mulcahey pointed up towards the Overlook. White mountain laurels were in bloom sticking out here and there in-between the hillside crevasses.

"Let's have one of your people scale the hillside and look for broken branches and fiber traces," McClure said.

"Already on it, sir," Mulcahey said.

"Alright. Good work, Mulcahey," McClure said. "I'll let you get back to supervising the transport of the remains." She nodded and walked back to her team.

"Trooper Drury? When you get back to the barracks, check the Missing Persons reports going back the last year. Start with the spring time frame? See what turns up. In the meantime, I'll check with ViCap."

"Yes sir."

McClure was referring to the Violent Criminal Apprehension Program, a unit of the FBI responsible for the analysis of serial violent and sexual crimes. Created in 1985 and headquartered in Quantico, Virginia, when it was realized that serial homicides could be linked by their signature aspects. It is designed to track and correlate information on violent crime, especially murder.

McClure looked back up at the Overlook.

"Whoever is responsible for this has been in the wind for at least a year. So, he's got a hell of a huge lead on us, but I still intend to close this case. The National Park Service would be reluctant to admit that this isn't the first time that a dead body's been dumped somewhere inside this secluded place."

Drury nodded and looked over at the SID team.

"I'd like to also question the hikers who found this guy's remains," Drury said. "Thanks to them, some family and friends will get some closure about the disappearance of a loved one. They should know the whole story."

"Agreed. And with any luck and good police work, in time we'll be able to tell them that we caught the sick son of bitch who did this. Let's get back topside and reopen Skyline Drive shall we?"

"Yes, sir."

Within an hour, cars with tourists were parked on Stony Man Overlook, enjoying the breath-taking scenery, amidst the ostensible presence of several police cars and a half-dozen State Troopers mulling about.

Chapter 1

The following cloudy day was Sunday. It was morning, and Marty Tate, the Sheriff of Dare County, was pulling into the Lost Colony Cove Marina in his unmarked cruiser. He had hastily left his wife Elizabeth before church services were concluded because his pager alerted him that his presence here was requested forthwith.

Through the front windshield he glanced at the scene of the homicide investigation stretched out before him. The S.I.D. vans were here along with several Dare County Sheriff's Department cars together with the van from the county morgue.

He pulled the car into the docking slip and put the car in park. To his left behind the yellow "Police: Do Not Cross" tape a gathering of reporters were setting up their video cameras for the live action feed "on location." They reminded Tate of the hungry gulls that were wandering around the docks in search of scraps. They irritated him, yet he understood that it was their job to report the news of a murder that they undoubtedly picked up from their police scanners. Murder was a rarity here, and therefore sensational news.

Marty Tate was 46 years old but looked younger. He stood just over six feet tall, and generally kept his weight under 220 pounds. He had thick brown hair, green eyes, bushy eyebrows and a thick mustache, and his hands were the size of a stone mason's. Tate was a former lieutenant with the North Carolina State Police, and six years ago he and Elizabeth and their two college-aged kids moved to Roanoke Island. Four years ago, he ran for and was elected Sheriff, and his re-election this fall was certain as he was running unopposed. He was highly skilled investigator who preferred to be in the field instead of riding a desk. He was popular and well-respected and successfully closed a disturbing serial murder case here a year ago.

Kenny Smith was standing on the dock with Officer Piper beside him. Kenny was his most distinguished and most trusted officer on his team. He was smart and self-effacing, and he had a habit of correcting his boss when Tate was speaking too generally, which he often was. Piper was the veteran police force Bloodhound. She appeared bored, and she yawned as Tate dismounted his vehicle.

"What've we got, Kenny," Tate barked as he approached.

"A dead body in the below decks cabin with a small caliber head shot wound right between the eyes." He handed Tate a steaming paper cup of Starbucks coffee.

"Nice boat," Tate said as he surveyed the imposing watercraft moored in front of him.

"Actually sir," Smith said "it's a yacht. About a 40 footer, I'd say."

Tate jerked his head away from the vessel to Smith.

"Look, Kenny, I've just arrived here on the scene wearing my Sunday go-to-meeting monkey suit; haven't had my first sip of coffee; and you're correcting my terminology already. Give me a break!" He took a pull on his coffee cup.

"It's a frickin' boat," he said as he panned the marina. "They're all just big, expensive boats."

Smith grinned.

"Well sir, there are all sorts of *boats* out here. Some are yachts like the one behind us, and there are some sailboats, schooners, skiffs, and sloops. Do you always swear this much after just leaving church?"

"On a morning like *this*? *Shit* yes... Who's our vic.?"

"A psychiatrist. Dr. Phillip McCleney. Runs – ran – a successful practice up in Kitty Hawk. We'll know more about his financials when the banks open up tomorrow, but it's fair to say that he looked to be doing very well given this yacht, the slip fees, and the membership to the marina and all. It's not cheap."

Tate nodded and looked back at the reporters and photographers.

"Anybody speak to *them* yet," he said.

"No sir. We thought that would be better left to you after you've had a preliminary examination of the scene."

"Okay," Tate said as he took another slug of caffeine. "What's the estimated time of death?"

"We're thinking between 10pm and midnight. We'll know more after we get him on the table and examine the stomach contents, etc., but the coroner's assistant says she's pretty sure based on the body temp..."

"O.K. Who called this in to us?"

"One of the security guards here at the marina. They got a call from McCleney's girlfriend who called and asked them to check the yacht as he was overdue for their usual early morning breakfast."

"Has she been notified?"

"Yes sir, but, we didn't give her any details. She's distraught enough as it is."

"I see," Tate said as he watched more media people arriving.

"There's something else."

"There's *always* something else."

"The on-board safe is empty, and the victim's wedding ring finger was amputated postmortem.

"Great," Tate said. "Swell... We've got another sicko on our hands. Have you found the missing finger?"

"Negative."

"The perp probably kept it as some sort of memento." He took one last pull on his coffee. "Did Piper come up with anything?"

Piper woofed gently at the sound of her name and looked up at Tate. Tate patted her on the head.

"No sir. There's no scent marker for her to work with. I just brought her along hoping that we'd get lucky. I'll put her in the car and then we can take a look around aboard the yacht."

"It's boat, Kenny. It's just a big...fucking...boat." He grinned back at Smith.

"Okay sir. You win. We'll take a look aboard the boat after I put Piper in the car."

"That's better. And thanks for the coffee. See you around, Piper."

Piper snuffled as Kenny Smith escorted her to the car that had the "K9 Unit" marker across its trunk, while Tate tossed his empty paper cup into the public trashcan and gathered his thoughts about what he would say to the press corps other than the thinnest veneer of facts.

An hour passed by. Crime scene technicians had located a spent .22 caliber shell casing inside the cabin. It was dusted for prints but none were found. Tate speculated that the killer wore gloves when he loaded his weapon. Following a first - hand look at the crime scene, Tate and Smith stood outside on the stern of Phillip McCleney's yacht.

"So, what are you thinking, Kenny?"

"If it wasn't for the amputated finger, on the surface it appears to be a run of the mill robbery/homicide."

"Maybe it was one of his patients," Tate said.

"I don't know about that. Most people who seek out some form of psychotherapy present no danger to other people. They're more liable to hurt themselves."

"Okay, but give me a definition of 'crazy.' Hell, for that matter, give me a definition of 'normal.' We have to include the possibility as one line of inquiry in our investigation."

"True. But, I highly doubt that he would see patients aboard this yacht. How many of his patients would even know that he owned one? He most likely would not share personal information with them."

"No, but if he posted pictures of this thing on Facebook, then just about anyone could find it here. This is the largest marina for these kinds of boats," Tate said.

Smith considered this and nodded.

"We'll be banging on the door of his practice tomorrow morning. At least we'll get more details on the kinds of people he was seeing. That sort of thing."

"Roger that."

"Let's check with ViCAP too first thing, to see if this wedding ring finger signature has turned up anyplace else? Maybe we have a frequent flier on our hands instead of a whack job's debut homicide committed on these Outer Banks."

"Got it. Anything else?"

Tate looked at his watch. "The usual," he said. "Make the necessary notifications to Dr. McCleney's kin folk as soon as you can?"

"You got it. Good luck with the Press," Smith said as he hiked his head in the direction of the reporters.

"I'll be my usual self with them, Kenny. Frustratingly brief, and obtuse as all hell," Tate said as he looked in their direction.

Kenny Smith smiled. "I'm sure that's *exactly* what they're expecting from you, sir."

Chapter 2

By 10:00 am the following Monday morning, Marty Tate and Kenny Smith were heading north on Route 158 outside of Kitty Hawk, having concluded a meagerly successful interview with Dr. Frederick Morrow - the late Dr. Phillip McCleney's business partner - at his clinic.

"Well, I wouldn't call that a *total* waste of our time," Smith said as he sat in the front passenger seat of the unmarked white Dodge Challenger.

Tate gave him a cursory glance as he sat behind the wheel. They were both wearing civilian clothes. They were on route to a face-to-face sit down interview with Ms. Anne Scarborough, McCleney's former fiancé.

"What exactly did we just learn from that high falootin' Ph.D. anyway?" Tate said. "I lost track of how many times he repeated "Patient/Doctor confidentiality." He pinned the accelerator to pass a slow moving Harris Teeter Markets semi-trailer truck.

"Well, we learned that McCleney's patients weren't bouncing-off-the-wall psychotics. Morrow said that the vast majority of the deceased's patients were couples undergoing marriage counseling."

"Wasn't McCleney *single?*" Tate asked rhetorically.

"You know that he was," Smith said as he looked out the passenger window glancing at the long row of restaurants and retail establishments that were getting busier with the advent of tourist season gaining on them.

"Don't you love irony, Kenny? For instance, our victim had no first - hand experience with matrimony and yet he had the nerve to be charging his patients $250 an hour for advice on how to stay happily married." Tate brushed his right hand towards the windshield as if he were swatting a fly.

"Being single didn't necessarily disqualify him from being a good therapist. And he was planning to marry Ms. Scarborough."

"Okay. I'll give you that. What else did we learn before I continue to digress further?"

"We learned that McCleney was successful, as we suspected. He paid the clinic's bills on time, his assistant's pay on time, and he didn't brag or boast about how well-off he was. His partner also confirmed that his yacht ownership was strictly privileged information."

"Uh huh. So where does that leave us?" Tate said.

"Unfortunately, at the same place that we were yesterday morning," Smith said. "We're still waiting for the M.E.'s official report, but, we know that one of Dr. McCleney's fingers was amputated postmortem. The empty safe on board his yacht is just a lame attempt to make it look like a robbery gone wrong. He was killed intentionally. And, we still don't know why, or who done it."

"Dr. McCleney's *wedding ring* finger was amputated postmortem," Tate said.

"Yes," Smith said with a tincture of gravity. "And now we know that the deceased was doing a lot of marriage counseling for the last couple of years. Jesus, you're sure as hell sounding like the suspicious son of a bitch that you truly are."

"It's a gift, and it's my job. But, now you're catching up with where I'm going. Besides, I can't afford to waste all that fancy profiler training that I took in Quantico a couple of years back. You neither."

Tate was referring to the eleven week National Academy Program which focuses on behavioral and forensic science, leadership development, as well as fitness training for selected police officers who have outstanding records of merit within their agencies. Tate and Smith were the respective top graduates in their classes. Tate continued.

"Most of what we learned from good Dr. Morrow was that the vast majority of our victim's patients had marriage problems."

Smith nodded.

"So, these patients were receiving therapy from a psychologist who had no wife. The still unknown suspect who aced McCleney last Saturday took the time to cut off McCleney's wedding ring finger postmortem before he fled the scene. Just say - in,' that's all." Tate spread out his fingers over the rim of the steering wheel and hiked his shoulders.

"And that's more than just a little too co - IN- incidental for you, eh boss?"

"You're damned straight it is," Tate said.

"The wedding ring finger amputation is a signature of the killer, alright. I can feel it. We can't rule out that it's a former patient just yet," Tate continued. "But, with the Doctor/Patient confidentiality thing, we don't even have a single name to go on. *Shit...*" He finished in exasperation.

"I don't know, Marty. If – and that's a *big* if – if you ask me, a patient discovered the good Dr. McCleney's history of being unmarried they felt what? Betrayed? They could just stop seeing him and ask for their money back. They could call him a con artist. Hell, they could even file an official complaint with the American Psychological Association. A person wouldn't have to whack the guy to get some sort of satisfaction. I respectfully don't see where you're going with that line of thinking."

"I don't know, either." Tate said. "Maybe I'm just thinking out loud. But, you and I both know that the amputated wedding ring finger is strongly symbolic. We don't know what the fuck it means, but the perpetrator sure as hell does."

"Looks like we're gonna' be right on time," Smith said, as he pointed to a sign that read, "Welcome to Southern Shores."

"Why don't you take the lead on this interview, boss?"

Tate looked over at Smith.

"Why? You're less intimidating to look at than me. Even though I am wearing my best Sunday-go-to-meetin' clothes," Tate said with a smile.

"Because *you're* a happily married man with two kids in college. That makes *you* the expert in the room when it comes to strong relationships. You more or less just said so yourself."

"Okay," Tate said. "And I'm glad that you used the term, 'strong.'"

"Why's that?"

"Because if you had used the term, 'perfect' I'd have to correct you. Just ask Lizbeth," Tate said, referring to his wife.

"Don't josh me, Marty. I've been around the two of you a lot over the last couple of years, and I'd have to say that Elizabeth worships the ground that you walk on."

"Oh contraire, Deputy Smith. It's *exactly* the other way around," he said with a smile. He continued.

"Alright. I'll take the lead on the interview. I'd like to focus most of my questions on how she met Phillip McCleney and about their relationship, as tactfully as I can. That's where I might need your help."

"Oh, you can be very tactful," Smith said. "When you try."

They pulled into the driveway of a two-story home; parked the car and cut the ignition.

Chapter 3

That same Monday morning found Mr. Richard Dolenz working in his office of the oceanfront cottage that he rented in Duck; a small coastal town in the northern Outer Banks that has a year-round population of around 350 souls, give or take.

He was seated at his desk behind his computer screen scrolling through the two dozen photos that he had snapped off at yesterday morning's hastily-called press conference at The Lost Colony Cove and Marina. Eventually he came across a satisfactory image of Dare County Sheriff Marty Tate wearing civilian clothes, surrounded by members of the media and law enforcement, making the announcement about the sudden and unexpected death of Dr. Phillip McCleney of Nags Head. Despite the press corps mercilessly hounding the sheriff for details about the "suspicious" death, Tate bore up well and said very little, as Dolenz remembered. Tate ended the interview assuring the assorted members of the local media that Dr. McCleney's death was under "active investigation," and that the answers to his office's questions would have to be satisfied first, before further details were released to them.

"He's as cool as a cucumber, that one is," Dolenz said aloud to himself in the empty cottage, as he considered the photo of Tate.

The local newspaper that Dolenz freelanced for would be expecting the photo within the hour so that it could accompany a story about the "suspicious" death in tomorrow's edition. He glanced over his desk to the coffee cup that was resting next to his mobile cell phone. He picked up the latter and held it to his ear.

"Yes," he said into the phone.

"Well, my dear boy. How are you this morning?" The voice belonged to Terry Grant, his closest friend since childhood days.

"I'm fine," Dolenz said. "But, you see I'm rather keen on getting an important piece of business tidied up before my paper's deadline, so I shan't be talking long."

"Well now. That's rather brusque, Dickie. Wouldn't you say?"

"Brusque?"

"Yes. Quite. Brusque in your manner of speech to the point of ungracious harshness."

Silence for a while.

"You shan't be talking long, you say," Grant finally spoke mockingly. "You might as well have said, 'piss off!'" He sounded irritated, and he continued.

"This after I settled a major score for you this past Saturday night, *Dickie*. I'm not hearing any appreciation or even affection on this end of the mobile, I daresay."

"Sorry," Dolenz finally offered. "It's just that I have quite a lot to be thinking through. Details regarding Saturday night and such, you see."

"Ah," Grant said sounding empathetic. "You just leave all that to your old, dear chum, Terry. Nothing's changed since we were lads. I'm still your one man cleanup crew. You can always count on me."

Dolenz stared out the window and spied a mourning dove bouncing back and forth on the railing of the outside deck, the sun shining brightly on its brown feathers.

"Sorry for sounding so harsh," he said. "It's just that…" His voice trailed off.

"Yes? Go on…"

"It's that Sheriff Tate. He worries me. He's awfully *cheeky*, that one is."

"Rubbish! You're not to be worried about him or anybody else for that matter. If I'm not worried, you shouldn't be either. By the way, old boy. Have you spoken to Mumsie lately?"

Dolenz's thoughts were re-directed quite abruptly, like a fast, forward moving vehicle that's been suddenly and violently slammed into reverse gear.

"Mother? Oh yes. I spoke with her yesterday. I thought I told you. Why do you ask?"

"Because it sounds to me that her relationship with that rather well-to-do bloke that she's been seeing could be moving steadily down the path to matrimony, that's why."

"Really? She didn't give me any indication of that," Dolenz said absent-mindedly as he sent his selected photograph of Sheriff Tate via cyberspace to his newspaper with the click of his mouse.

"That's because *she's* the one who's playing it cheeky. And, with *you*, Dickie, I daresay. Why, widowed for decades after she lost her hubby… Up until now I always assumed that she'd remain a spinster."

"I really must be ringing off now," Dolenz said. "You understand."

"Ah, yes of course. That deadline that you spoke of. Very well. I'll stay in touch. Cheerio! Bye for now, Richard."

"Bye," Dolenz said after he traded his mobile phone for his cup of coffee. He strolled into the kitchen and perused the calendar that was hanging on the wall by the refrigerator. He set his coffee down on a table and stared more carefully at today's date, which had his scribbling on it.

"Ah! Very good," he said aloud in a strong voice. "Mother's monthly stipend will be deposited into the account today. Thanks ever so much, Mum," he said as he winked at the calendar and turned back towards his office.

Strolling by the hallway bathroom, he walked in, turned on the light, and studied himself in the mirror. He stood exactly six feet tall, slim but athletic in build, with lithe, toned muscles that could be seen swelling through the short-sleeved powder blue polo shirt that he was wearing. His shoulders and upper torso were very well defined. He flexed his right arm the way he'd seen it done by bodybuilders on TV and he smiled. His teeth were sparkling. He had a full crop of wavy brown hair that he kept brushed to the side as he looked at his dazzling blue eyes staring back at him in the looking glass.

"Ah… Vanity is the flatterer of the soul," he said aloud before he turned off the light and returned to his office.

"On to the next piece of business, shall we?" he said as he clicked on his mouse and opened a website. His website. "Sea Side Wedding Photography, LLC," the top banner read. The landing page of the website displayed a variety of first-rate sunrise and sunset wedding pictures of happy couples and their colorful bridal parties. At the bottom of the page, the text read:

"Please click here in order to discover what sets us apart from the competition, when it comes to capturing the start of your happily-ever-after moments."

He smiled when he found that five, fresh new inquiries had come in since the weekend. He eagerly picked up his phone again and began the sales calls to the new, prospective clients.

Chapter 4

Situated on the banks of the Currituck Sound on the north end of the Waterfront Shops in Duck was the popular lunch and dinner spot called The Brown Pelican restaurant. Frederick Douglass Books, the head chef, together with the owner, Paul Treadwell were preparing to open the doors for the lunch crowd when Megan Treadwell emerged from the office which was located down a short hallway from the hostess station where Books and Paul were standing.

Paul's wife and co-owner of the restaurant was attractive. She stood 5'7" tall, had a curvaceous figure, and shoulder length brown hair that she wore loosely today. Her blue eyes seemed to sparkle whenever she caught sight of Paul, if she was in a jovial mood. Such was the case today.

"So, who's buying lunch today?" Paul said as he stepped away from the hostess station. Paul stood 6'2" tall and had a slim figure. He was in his mid-forties and fit, and still had a full crop of wavy brown hair which he kept neatly trimmed. Back in his home state of Ohio he was a seasoned robbery homicide detective.

"Kim is," Megan said, referring to her lunch date and one of her favorite friends on these Outer Banks.

"She sure better be," Books said with a grin that revealed his perfect white teeth. "I mean, with all the advice that you give her about the various men in her life, you ought to be charging her by the hour. That girl sure do talk your ears off," he said as he shook his head in jest.

Books was a tall, 6'3" ex-Marine Gunnery Sgt., who was an expert in hand-to-hand combat and various forms of martial arts. He had also become the closest personal friend of the Treadwell's since they bought the place three years back after moving down to the Outer Banks permanently from their home state of Ohio. "Gunny," as he was known had also saved Megan's life one year ago, as she nearly became the last victim of a vindictive serial killer, who had stalked her meticulously for five months before he made his move on her.

Like Paul, Books was in his mid-forties, and was still searching for "Ms. Right." Thanks to his vast culinary skills, he

23

made this restaurant the most popular in Duck. During the "in season," savvy repeat guests knew to call for a dinner reservation up to one month in advance.

"It's true that she hasn't had much luck with men," Megan said. "It seems a shame that she hasn't come across level-headed guys such as the two of you. Then again Gunny, it's been awhile since you've been in a serious relationship," she said as she winked at him.

"True dat," Gunny said with a smile. "I'm about as picky with my women friends as I am about my food."

"I'd buy that explanation," Paul said with a slight chuckle.

Megan walked over and stood on her toes and gave Paul a kiss on his cheek and said, "I'll be back before you finish the lunch service. Then, I'll take the Jeep back to the house and take Brandy for a beach walk." She was referring to the couple's year-round home in the Sea Ridge subdivision just a few miles north of the restaurant as well as the couple's six year old chocolate - brown Labrador retriever.

"Sounds good, hon," he said. "Where are you and Kim having lunch?"

"The Roadhouse, of course. I'm walking. It's too nice a day to drive." Outside it was sunny with temperatures in the 70's.

"The Roadhouse do serve a mean crab cake sandwich," Books said with what Megan thought was a slight tincture of jealousy. "Give Amy my best and tell her that I'll be by soon?"

He was referring to Amy Garland, The Roadhouse's manager and owner. The restaurant was just a short walk south of the Brown Pelican on the east side of Duck Road, the northern section of highway N.C. 12 that snakes its way four miles through the small coastal town.

"I will," Megan said. "She really loves it whenever you stop by to talk about the food business, and to share personal recipes. She says she's learned a lot from you."

Book smiled and nodded.

"Okay you two. Carry on, and I'll see you later," Megan said as she opened the front screened door and made her way past the incoming lunch crowd, cut across the Waterfront Shop's parking lot, and turned south on Duck Road at a quickstep.

24

Within a few minutes, she crossed the street and arrived at her destination. The Roadhouse Bar and Grill was once a private residence, and one of the first houses built in Duck in 1932. The weathered wood exterior has a porch where diners can enjoy the great food alfresco during the good weather days.

Megan walked through the front door and could make out the strains of soft jazz coming from the small overhead speakers. The odor of crab meat and Old Bay seasoning filled the air. To her left was a small bar with a half-dozen stools and just beyond was the open kitchen. To her right were three booths partially enclosed with split pine rails. Kim was seated inside the first one closest to the entrance.

"You beat me to it," Megan called out. "I hope you weren't waiting long?"

"Nope. Just got here a minute ago," Kim said. They hugged, then Megan took the seat opposite her friend. Kim Montgomery was an attractive blond in her early thirties. She was 5' 10" tall but appeared taller due to her straight posture and slim figure. Like Megan, she wore her hair at shoulder length. Her eyes were emerald green. She had a long face with high cheek bones, a strong jaw, and a slight cleft in her chin.

Megan often noticed how men would stare at them both whenever they were together. They met two years ago at the health club near Milepost 1 in Southern Shores. Kim had a job at Coastal Diamonds and Gems Jewelry store in Nags Head.

They each ordered beer and the crab cake sandwich platter that was served with fresh coleslaw, ginger, homemade kettle - cooked potato chips, and an enormous dill pickle. When the food arrived they continued their small talk about their latest shopping finds, work, good books to read on the beach, and eventually the talk turned to Kim's new guy friend. They ordered another round of beer and placed a dessert order for Key Lime pie.

"So," Megan said with a slight grin. "Who's this new guy that you wanted to tell me about?"

"I've only gone out with him a few times over the past couple of weeks," Kim said as she peered over at their server who was putting in their beer order at the bar.

"Where'd you meet him? At our health club?" Kim looked back at her.

"Oh, *God* no. You've seen the guys at that club. If you ask me, they're mostly married lechers pretending to be single. No, no. I met this guy online."

Megan pursed her lips and frowned, signaling puzzlement.

"You were introduced to this guy on the internet?"

"Yeah," Kim said with a smile. Their second round of beers arrived. Megan took a quick pull on her long-neck instead of pouring it into the chilled mug.

"Didn't you meet the last two... I think that you called them '*losers*'... online? You *do* remember the classic definition of insanity, don't you dear?"

Kim placed her elbows on the table and waved her hands in front of her face as if she were warding off the oncoming criticism.

"Yeah, yeah. I know. Doing the same thing over and over again and expecting a different result. I get it," she said. She did the same as Megan and drank a quick swig straight from the bottle.

"I found those two losers on a totally different online dating website that I swear, I'll never use again. This new website that I found is devoted to people who are searching for a serious and committed relationship."

"Uh huh," Megan said as she drew out the 'huh' part of the expression for an extra second.

Their server came back to their table.

"How are the two of you doing?"

Kim and Megan smiled and nodded.

"Okay. Great! Just signal me when you both want that dessert order?"

More smiles and nods. The server walked to the next booth.

"Anyway..." Kim said. "This guy's name is David Wiggins. He's young, charming, witty, and most especially very good looking. Here... I'll show you his picture on my phone."

She reached into her bag and retrieved what looked like a white Samsung Android, pushed a button, accessed the restaurant's Wi-Fi, then swiped the screen a couple of times before turning around it towards Megan.

"Nice phone," Megan said. "Is it new?"

"Yes. David gave it to me the other day. I just love it. It's such a huge upgrade from my old one." She turned the front of the phone around so that Megan could see it.

Megan quickly studied the image of a smiling man, probably in his late twenties, with sparkling teeth, and thick brown hair brushed to the right side of his face. His dazzling eyes were deep blue.

"He's cute," Megan said. Kim put her phone away. "What's he do for a living around here?"

"That's one of the things about him that I don't really understand," Kim said. "He claims that he's a venture capitalist. He, together with some co-investors, loan money to promising start-up firms. I really don't know or understand how that all works."

"Me, neither," Megan said. "I'd guess that you'd have to be 'charming and witty' to be a good one though."

Kim looked down at her beer and crossed her arms on the table.

"What is it?" Megan said.

Kim looked back at her.

"Well, he is fun to be around but there are a couple of things that seem odd to me, that's all."

"Starting with…what?"

"It's that I've never, ever seen him use a debit or a credit card. I mean, *ever*. He pays cash everywhere we go. Even when he puts gas in to that expensive car that he leases or owns outright. You know how paperless society is today. Doesn't that seem odd to you, too?"

Megan nodded with a neutrality to her facial expression.

"If your gut tells you that there's something off or odd about another person or their behavior, then I'd say pay extra attention to that. Because that's all that matters. What *you* feel." She took another drink of beer.

Kim nodded, looking away.

"Anything else?" Megan said. Kim returned her gaze to her.

"Well. I've never been to his house or apartment yet. I guess that's not too odd since we're not at that stage in our relationship. But, whenever I ask him where he lives he just smiles and says, 'All will be revealed in due course.' Isn't *that* a little weird?"

"Does he know where *you* live?"

"Oh sure. He's picked me up there when we've gone out. I've never asked him to stay or anything like that." They both finished their beers and then signaled the server for their desserts.

"I don't know," Megan said. "You said that this website is for people looking for a serious and committed relationship. Maybe he's taking things cautiously if he's been burned before? I don't know. It does seem odd."

"Yeah," Kim said.

"Why don't you bring him by the Pelican for lunch or dinner sometime? Paul has a solid, finely-honed bullshit detector that he's refined during his years as a cop. It's second only to mine, that is," Megan said with a grin.

Kim smiled and let out a small laugh.

"I did tell David about you two and your place, and he agreed that we should go and soon."

"Good," Megan said. "Here comes our dessert. Weren't the sandwiches fabulous?"

"As always," Kim said as two chilled plates were set before them, and soon their conversation turned to planning a mani/pedi session at the Sanderling Resort and Spa a few miles north of here.

The check arrived and Kim snapped it off the table.

"You don't have to pay for the both of us," Megan said. "Let's split it?"

"No, I insist," Kim said as she shook her head and got a credit card out of her purse.

"Besides, you gave me some good advice about David."

"I did?"

"Yes you did. You told me to pay more attention to my own feelings. Instead, I think that I've been spending too much time thinking of ways that I might appeal more to him."

"I think that you came to that conclusion all by yourself, girlfriend."

"No. I needed to talk some things through with you. You're great. Thanks a lot friend."

"What are older friends for? Thanks for the compliment. And the great lunch. I'm gonna' head home and take Brandy out for a good beach hike and work off this food. How about you?"

"I'm heading to the health club with the same idea. I have a date with my favorite stationary bike."

Megan left the tip and they were on their way.

Miles away and moments ago, Terry Grant was sitting in his spacious living room with his laptop computer turned on. He was enjoying his time as a cyber voyeur. He smiled as he watched and listened - in to the live conversation between Kim and Megan. Indeed, David Wiggins had given Kim her new Android phone, but, at *Terry's* suggestion. And, only after he had taken the liberty of going into the phone's Settings menu and toggled a switch that overrode the system default, in order to allow the installation of apps from "unknown sources." Just a few moments ago, Kim Montgomery honestly thought that she was logging on to the restaurant's legitimate Wi-Fi, when in fact it was a ghost version sent to her phone by Terry Grant. It's what clever hackers like himself refer to as "spoofing."

All smartphones are essentially supercomputers that contain in them more technology than what was contained in the Apollo spacecraft that travelled to the moon and back. Over 800 global cell phone companies are a part of "signaling system seven," otherwise known as SS7. The problem with SS7 is that holes can be found in its defenses, and exploited by global national security agencies as well as sophisticated hackers such as Terry Grant. Once he got hold of a cell phone number he could expertly breach an opening into SS7, and he'd be "in" as he was now.

Now, through Kim Montgomery's camera on her new phone, he was able to listen and watch her and Megan Treadwell covertly, from the comfort of his living room. Had he wished, he could have accessed all of her e-mails as well as her account I.D., together with the credit card data that she used for that account. However, this wasn't necessary. Not yet, anyway.

"Nice phone," Megan said. "Is it new?"

"Yes. David gave it to me the other day."

"He's cute," Megan said. Then the images of Kim and Megan went black on the laptop screen.

Terry Grant closed the lid of his computer and chortled out loud.

"He *IS* cute, I dare say," he said. "And quite a clever bloke he is, too, with me doing all the thinking for him."

A memory began to unspool in his brain of the time when he insisted that David present Ms. Anne Scarborough with a new Android phone, a couple of months back. David didn't want to at first, but good 'ol Terry persuaded him to give it a go. And it all turned out for the better because of it.

After all, thanks to that phone, Terry Grant was able to learn of and get to know Dr. Phillip McCleney – vicariously of course – before he murdered him up close and in person at the Lost Colony Cove Marina last Saturday. As an additional bonus, he even got to watch and listen to Anne Scarborough's grieving calls later that evening when she learned of Phillip's demise. Now *that* was totally delicious! Watching and listening to that delirious *bitch*, as she droned on and on to her friends about how much she *loved* Phil, and what a *soul mate* he was to her, and who could have *done* such a horrible thing, and such and such, and so on, and so on, and so on...

"*Fuck* her," he said in a loud voice, as he raised his right arm and made an obscene gesture, flipping a "bird" in the air to no one. His mind and his gaze returned to his surveillance equipment.

"You know, the only difference between men and boys are the price of their toys. I'm hungry. I wonder what's in the fridge for lunch?" He said, as he got up from the couch and trotted off to the kitchen.

Chapter 5

Marty Tate and Kenny Smith were back at the Dare County Sheriff's Office located in Manteo on Driftwood Drive. Manteo is the county seat of Dare, and was named after a native-American Croatoan tribe member who was brought to London in 1584 by the early English colonists, who had established America's very first colony on Roanoke Island. The mystery of what became of "The Lost Colony," is still speculated, and has been the centerpiece of an annual symphonic drama that has been re-enacted at Roanoke Island's Waterside Theater since the 1930's.

During the course of their interview with Anne Scarborough they had learned that she had met Dr. Philip McCleney through a dating website known as "Happily-Ever-After.com." After they had learned all that they could about the late psychiatrist, it was time to get back to base and review the ViCap database.

They were in Tate's office where Marty sat at his desk clattering away on his computer keyboard. Smith sat opposite him reviewing the notes from this morning's interviews. After a few moments, Tate's assistant Peggie popped her head into his open office door.

"I'm heading over to Stripers to pick up a takeout sandwich for lunch. Would y'all like me to bring you back something as well?"

Peggie had been Marty's assistant ever since he first took office. A vivacious, 63-year-old blond and blue-eyed southern belle who didn't look a day past 50. She was an exercise nut her whole life and she tried to run two miles every day weather permitting.

"How about a couple of shrimp baskets?" Tate said as he looked across to Kenny Smith who nodded his head with some obvious vigor.

"You won't get any back talk from me on that suggestion," Smith said. "It's my turn to treat," he said as he reached for his wallet and produced two twenty-dollar bills and handed them over to Peggie.

After she left on her food run, Tate spoke after he made another keystroke.

31

"Well, well, well...," he said. "It looks as if our unknown subject is a repeat customer whose last known location was at the scene of a killing near Charlottesville one year ago. Take a look at this," he said as he got up and out of his chair to afford Smith a chance to get a good look at the computer screen.

"Charlottesville, huh?" Smith said as his eyes focused on the information and photos displayed on the database. The images included photos of a young man in his prime, together with his decayed remains that were photographed at Shenandoah National Park. Smith began to read aloud what he was seeing even though he knew that Tate had already assessed the available data.

"The deceased's name was Kevin Berkley, a senior about to graduate with high honors from U.V.A... Was reported missing one year ago in May by his family and his fiancé', Ms. Mary Brennen. Berkley's remains were discovered last month – as you said – along the base of the Skyline Drive. Cause of death ruled a homicide. Took one right between the eyes, courtesy of a .22 caliber at close range. Yadda, yadda, yadda... What else?"

"Keep scrolling down," Tate said. "You'll find it."

"Son of a gun," Smith said out loud. "The vic's wedding ring finger was amputated postmortem. Coincidence?"

Tate shrugged. "Not likely. You know how I feel about coincidences in a homicide. The Virginia case is listed as open/unsolved," Tate said.

"Yep," Smith said. "It's under active investigation by the Virginia staties. Do you happen to know this Lt. Jared McClure who is listed as the lead investigator?" Smith looked up from the monitor to see Tate nodding his head.

"That's affirmative," Tate said. "Years back when I was with the N.C. state police, McClure and I served on a multi-state jurisdictional task force. We were trying to shut down the drug traffic which originated up north in Cincinnati. His guys and ours brought in a lot of major scumbags at the state borders."

Smith stood up and returned to his original chair. Tate sat back down behind his desk again.

"McClure sounds like a straight shooter," Smith said. "What's he like to work with? After all, I'll be getting acquainted with him soon."

"McClure is whip smart, and probably the best marksman in the State of Virginia," Tate said. "And very best of all, he's not a *dick*."

Smith nodded and grinned as he listened to one of Tate's favorite and familiar descriptions of men that he admired.

"And who are the best shots that you've seen here in the Banks?" Smith asked.

"Paul Treadwell and Gunny Books are two of the best I've seen." Tate said. Smith nodded.

"You're no slouch yourself, Marty. You've won every competition that I've seen you shoot in."

"It's a gift," Tate said with a smirk on his face as he picked up his desktop phone and dialed the number for the Virginia State Police.

Chapter 6

Nestled within a lavish manicured landscape that exudes the grandeur of a Virginia country estate is the historic Williamsburg Inn. One of the finest luxury hotels in North America, built at the behest of John D. Rockefeller Jr. in 1937, the Williamsburg Inn has welcomed hundreds of VIP's across the years, twice hosting Queen Elizabeth and Prince Phillip.

It was evening and growing dark. The high dew point exceeded the high outdoor temperature making the atmosphere sultry, tropical, and typical along the Virginia peninsula. Seated at a table inside the Inn's air-conditioned Rockefeller Room restaurant were Julia Dolenz and her newly-engaged consort, Mr. Reginald White. He, a British ex-pat and a highly successful divorce attorney is the founder and head of a thriving law firm with offices a stone's throw from the College of William and Mary.

Formal dining at the Rockefeller Room was a special experience for those who could afford it, and between them, Julia and Reggie had amassed a sizable nest egg as a result of his exorbitant billable hours together with Julia's sizable inheritance. She received it shortly after the death of her first husband when they lived in England over two decades ago. Her husband took suddenly ill and passed away due to what was described at the inquest as "...heart failure due to inexplicable causes." Since Scotland Yard could find no evidence of skullduggery on Julia's part she was left a free woman. However, not long after the inquest she became the focus of rumors and scandalous speculation. In her quaint and quiet neighborhood in the suburbs of London she became known as 'The Black Widow' within gossip circles. Deeming this to be an unsuitable environment in which to raise her very young son Richard, she left England and settled in a grand home in the heart of Williamsburg.

Soft conversations mingled with laughter and the occasional tinkle of genuine sterling silverware against expensive china was a part of the ambiance of the Rockefeller Room. A pianist began to play the first notes of the jazz classic, "Misty," made famous by Johnny Mathis. The formal attire and jewelry worn by the diners projected an aura of pedigree and privilege, and Julia and her Reggie

34

sat dressed to the nines enjoying each other's company at a table situated at their usual spot near large, curved floor - to- ceiling windows which overlooked the lush and expansive Golden Horseshoe Golf Course.

"Have you had a busy day, lovey?" Julia said as the sommelier left their table in order to retrieve the wine selection that Reggie had made.

"Not especially," Reggie said. "At least, not for a Monday. The young Mr. Steele keeps pestering me about a partnership."

"He *is* assiduous, that one is," Julia said.

"Yes he is, I dare say."

"What did you tell him?"

"The same thing that I've told him a half-dozen other times. That as a Senior Associate he's being compensated as much as an income, non-equity partner, and unless he brings in double the fees he's collecting today, then I have no compulsion to share the firm's profits with him."

The sommelier brought the wine to the table, opened it expertly with his corkscrew, and then handed the cork to Reggie. Reggie passed the cork under his nostrils and nodded and the sommelier poured a small dram of wine into his glass for him to sample. Reggie did so approvingly, and the sommelier poured exactly four ounces of red wine into each of their glasses, wished them *bon appetite* then left. Julia lifted up her glass.

"To us," she toasted.

"To us indeed, luv," Reggie said as he raised his glass in kind.

"I'm so looking forward to shopping for my wedding ring with you tomorrow, Reg. That was so very thoughtful of you not to have made a selection without my consultation."

He chuckled.

"Well, I know my Julia," he chortled. "Making a selection independent of your opinion would never do. So, we're off to *The Precious Gemstone* at ten o'clock tomorrow?"

Julia nodded in a show of anticipation and beamed a smile. Reggie was referring to her favorite, local jewelry store located in Colonial Williamsburg's Merchants Square. At age 46, Julia could certainly still pass for a woman in her mid-thirties. Petite in height and weight, she had a trim athletic build. Her girlfriends at the health

35

club who were classic movie fans all remarked that she seemed to bear a rather strong resemblance to a young Audrey Hepburn. She had brown, shoulder-length hair that was tied up in a bun. Her arched eyebrows rested above her large and striking hazel eyes that often appeared to shift in color from brown to green. She fancied all kinds of athletics, loved horses and excelled at Dressage. She also held an 'expert level' markswoman's ranking in small arms fire at her all- women's shooting club, which was scheduled to compete in a handgun championship against members of the Virginia State Police in a couple of weeks.

Her consort had just turned fifty, but like Julia, he appeared younger in age. He had wavy brown hair and blue eyes. Tall and fit, he relished in the sport of tennis and he frequently played doubles with other attorneys on the courts that belonged to the Williamsburg Inn's Tennis Club.

Two hours later, having finished their meal, they were enjoying an after-dinner drink of Benedictine and Brandy. Reggie cleared his throat, sipped a small dram of his B&B, and then spoke.

"Have you had the time, darling, to give any thoughts to the matter that we discussed about Richard's future allowance?"

"I have indeed," Julia said. "And you'll be pleased to know that I agree with you, dear. Thirty seven hundred quid a month has been an outrageous allowance that I've been granting him. I'm sure that he's been able to live the Playboy life with that income, together with whatever he earns as a photographer. I'll be sure to call him on my mobile tomorrow and break the news to him. Beginning next month his allowance will be cut in half. On the following month, another cut of half that amount and so on and so on until he will have to be completely independent of the monthly stipend. Instead, we'll place a fair sum in a trust account for his future expenditures for when we're both gone."

"I know that we'd be doing the right thing with that, dearest. After all, he'll stand to receive a very generous inheritance. In the meantime, he'll have to be more frugal and learn to live within his means. He is after all, grown up and graduated from college and all that. It's not as if we're telling him to bugger off."

"When he was very young, I thought that I'd enjoy being a single mother, but as he reached the end of his grade school years, I

36

wanted to have my own life. So, instead of placing him in a local high school, I sent him off to Christchurch."

"The coed boarding school?"

"Yes. I thought that the experience would instill some discipline in him, but it didn't. When he graduated he wanted to attend William and Mary here in town, but I told him no. I told him that if he wanted to have his room and board and tuition completely paid that he'd have to attend The University of Virginia."

"He must have had good grades in order to attend either." Reggie said.

"Oh yes," Julia said. "Richard has always been a very intelligent and clever boy."

She looked directly into Reggie's eyes and smiled.

"Let's *do* move on to other topics, lovey? I shan't spend the rest of the evening talking about Richard."

"Yes, yes, yes. Let's... Just one curiosity though?"

"Of course, Reggie. What is it?"

"Well... How do you anticipate that Richard will take this news?"

"Oh not well, not well at all," Julia said as she waived her left arm in the air dismissively. "He's gone out of his way to remind me over the years of how many times that I've said 'no' to many of his wishes. I dare say that he'll hate me more after I break the news to him. That is, if hating me more is even possible for him."

"Really dear, I don't wish to drive another wedge between you and your only son."

"Don't worry Reggie," Julia said as she took a substantial pull on her B&B and drained the glass. "I'll make sure that he understands that our intention is to strengthen his *future* inheritance. In the meantime, as you said, he'll have to learn to be more responsible with his money, and not to be tied to my purse strings for the rest of his adult life, that's all."

"But, you still think that he'll hate you for saying so?"

"Oh, of *course*," Julia said. "Like mother, like son." She spread her hands over the white linen tablecloth. "Both he and I have never fancied the delay of gratification."

She beamed a broad smile.

"Speaking of gratification..." Julia said, as she let her flirtatious innuendo drift across the table to a smiling Reggie. She slipped her hands over his.

In the background, the pianist began to play the soft, opening chords to another Johnny Mathis favorite, *"Chances Are."*

Chapter 7

Two days following their discovery of the open unsolved homicide that had taken place one year ago in The Shenandoah National Park, Kenny Smith and Marty Tate had driven to Charlottesville, or "C-Ville," as the natives refer to it, in order to hold a "I'll show you mine, then you show me yours" meeting with Lt. Jared McClure and Trooper Fred Drury.

McClure and Drury provided Tate and Smith with a copy of the file that had started out as a missing person's case, and was now a homicide investigation. McClure and Drury were presently compiling a murder book which included crime scene photographs and sketches, forensic reports, transcripts of their notes and witness interviews.

Tate and Smith had done the same with their open homicide case of Dr. Phillip McCleney at the Lost Colony Cove Marina. They shared what the Dare County ballistics team had just recently revealed about the type of weapon used in the crime; a .22 caliber handgun, most likely an automatic. This conclusion was reached after examining the remains of the bullet found in the skull of the victim, as well as the shell casing that was discovered aboard McCleney's yacht. The shell casing had also been examined for fingerprints but none were found. The medical examiner also felt that the victim's wedding ring finger was most likely removed with sharp pruning shears.

McClure told Tate and Smith that the M.E. in Charlottesville concluded that Kevin Berkley had been shot execution style, also with a .22, given the diameter of the entry wound. In the spirit of cooperation and without regard to state boundaries and jurisdictions, the men freely exchanged additional information and tentative theories about their cases. McClure also noted and provided the names of those individuals who were interviewed one year ago shortly after the reported disappearance of Kevin Berkley. McClure's intention was to locate and re – interview as many of these individuals as possible in the light of new facts and circumstances surrounding the case.

At the end of the meeting, given the strong signature of the murderer, they all felt confident that the individual who had killed

Kevin Berkley in Virginia was also the same individual who had killed Phillip McCleney, one year later this month, in the Outer Banks.

When their two-hour-plus meeting was concluded, Smith returned to Manteo and Tate drove to Williamsburg in order to visit with his son, Robert E., who was attending summer classes at the College of William and Mary. Marty had phoned ahead and told his son that he would treat him to lunch at one of their favorite, upscale bistros in Merchants Square called The Red Talon.

According to the locals, if a kid could afford to attend William and Mary, then they certainly could afford a lunch at The Red Talon. Therefore, it didn't surprise Marty to see a smattering of the younger crowd enjoying the first-rate grub when he walked inside the restaurant from St. Francis Street. Above the bar there was a large, flat-screen TV which featured muted old black and white cartoons such as "Tom and Jerry," as well as classic television episodes of Julia Child's "The French Chef" series that originally aired in 1963.

Marty smiled as he recalled how he and Elizabeth enjoyed watching Julia Child on the big screen whenever they came over to mainland Virginia in order to visit their son Robert. The aroma of this establishment was always enticing, and Marty was debating whether he'd have beef or fish when he spotted his son, who was waving from a table situated towards the rear of the restaurant which faced a stately brick courtyard and a parking lot.

Robert E. Tate was tall like his dad. His hair was light brown and his eyes were violet like his mother's. He was wearing a William and Mary polo shirt with the college's colors of green and gold and silver over cargo pants and open – toed sandals. His backpack was on the chair beside him. He shoved a textbook inside it as his father approached the table. He had been named after Marty's father, a posthumously decorated Army sniper who died valiantly during the Vietnam War. Both Tate's were also named in honor of Robert E. Lee, the father figure of the Lost Cause of the South's "War of Northern Aggression."

They shook hands and hugged before they both sat down.

"It's great seeing you, Dad," Robert said with a smile.

"Likewise, son," Marty said as he smiled back.

The server placed the menus on the table and said he'd give them a few minutes to decide on their order.

"Are you still buying us lunch?" Robert asked.

"I don't know," Marty said looking serious. He pursed his lips. "How are your grades?"

Robert gave him a breakdown of excellent grades for all subject matters that he was studying at the college.

"Well then...," Marty said as he slapped his son on the shoulder. "Hell YES I'm buying you lunch! Your mom is going to be thrilled when I tell her the good news."

Robert bowed his head slightly with a grin on his face.

"Actually," he said slowly. "I just texted her the good news before you got here in order to bolster the odds of a free lunch. Here. Take a look at what she texted back." He held up his smartphone so that his father could read the message.

Marty looked down and squinted his eyes. The message read:

With grades that outstanding, be sure to tell your father to buy you WHATEVER you want for lunch, and tell him I said so! :-)

Marty nodded and chuckled with approval. "Yes, dear," Marty said to the phone. "Let's order."

After studying their menus, Robert ordered a Blackened Fish Reuben together with a regular iced tea. Marty selected the Pressed French Dip with steak fries and a mango – flavored iced tea.

The lunch and the conversation between them was excellent. The table was cleared and they had fresh drinks set before them as Marty waited for the tab.

"So," Marty said. "You haven't told me what's bothering you."

Robert looked at him with a measure of surprise on his face, then he smiled.

"I forgot that in addition to being my Dad that you're a highly trained investigator. I don't know why I bother trying to hide anything from you. It's never worked in the past."

Marty smiled back.

"And I'm *sure* that at inconvenient times when you were growing up, that was a real bitch," he said, still smiling.

"Copy that," Robert said as he nodded. You'll be wanting an answer to your question, I suppose."

"Uh huh," Marty said as he took a small pull on his iced tea. The restaurant lunch crowd was thinning out.

"Well, by fall term, the college would really like me to declare a major."

"You'll be a sophomore. I seem to recall that was the time I declared *mine* back in the dark ages at North Carolina State."

Robert chuckled.

"You always knew that you were going to major in Criminal Justice, just like you knew that you were going to play college football."

"True."

Marty waited. The bill arrived. Marty placed a credit card on top, and the server picked it up and went away again.

"I don't know what I should do," Robert said as he shook his head slightly.

"There's a lot of that going around," Marty said. He waited some more for his son to gather his thoughts. He was simultaneously wondering what he'd be doing next with his homicide investigation. Someone dropped a plate back in the kitchen.

"My professors all tell me that I have the makings for a great lawyer. That I should finish my undergrad studies here, then head off to some fancy law school and then take the bar." He shook his head and took a sip on his iced tea. "Too much time in school, and too much money spent, is what I say to that."

"A lot of lawyers make good money," Marty said.

"I know. Especially if you become a defense attorney."

"I *hate* defense attorneys," Marty said with a smile.

"I know," Robert said.

"So what do you tell your professors?" Marty said.

"I tell them that my favorite subject is political science, and that I'd like to work on a congressman's or a senator's staff when I graduate."

"Okay," Marty said. "Then what?"

"Then I'd run for elected office."

"I hate politicians," Marty said. He smiled back at his son again.

"I know. But, Dad. Face it. *You're* an elected official."

"Yes. But, I'm no politician."

"I think that Mom and Sis and I, and everyone on your staff, together with the entire citizenry of Dare County, North Carolina, gets that." He winked at his Dad and smiled again.

"When did you first know that you wanted to be a cop?"

"You already know the answer to that one, Robert. The deputy who rescued my cat Socks, who was stuck up a tree when I was a little boy. That deputy was my hero."

"I know. I remember. I just think it must have been so cool to know what you wanted to do for the rest of your life when you were just a little boy," Robert said.

"And it's *not* cool to be conflicted going into your sophomore year? I disagree. Son, I think that it's very cool that your professors see so much potential in you, as does your family that you just mentioned. You'll figure it out in due time. You want to hear what some wise person once told *me*?"

"Sure. I'd love to hear it. Shoot."

"A purpose... Is not something that you find. Instead, it will find you. But not a moment before you're ready for it."

Robert sat back in his chair and nodded.

"Wow. That's deep," Robert said. "Who told you that?"

"Your Grandmother. My Mom."

A small tear welled up inside of Robert's right eye.

"How cool. Way to go, Grandma! You must miss her a lot, Dad."

"She *was* cool. And yes. I miss her every day. Goddamned cancer."

They were both quiet for a while. The check was paid. Marty looked at his watch. It was time for him to head back to Manteo.

They both stood and headed to the door that led to the parking lot. They hugged, then Marty headed for his car. Robert following him.

"What's happening back at the cop shop?" Robert asked.

Marty opened the driver's door of the car, leaned against it and looked back at his son. He put on his sunglasses.

"A double homicide investigation has just opened up."

"Shit," Robert said as he shook his head.

"Yep," Marty said. "And unless we catch this guy soon, I'm positive that he'll do it again."

43

Richard put the phone away and looked back at the two women who were both sitting up surveying the beach. He finished his beer. When the very cute one turned her head his way he waved and smiled. She raised her right hand high in the air and gave him the finger with a scowl on her face. Richard nodded at the obscene gesture and looked back out at the surf. He snorted and shook his head.

"Quite alright," he said out loud. "She's probably a dyke anyway."

Then he reached into his cooler for beer number three.

Chapter 9

Two weeks later on a Saturday, at a Virginia State Police outdoor qualifying range in Newport News, Julia Dolenz together with Reginald White and various members of her all-women Williamsburg shooting team were assembled for a competition match against the best shooters of the State Police. Both sides had turned this into a charity event, and a handsome sum had been raised for the Widows and Orphans Fund of the Virginia State Police. Several men and women officers of different rank represented the V.S.P. including last year's top trophy winner, Lt. Jared McClure. McClure was considered the heavy favorite to repeat last year's near perfect performance. The Williamsburg women, equally paired against the officers for today's match, also had their favorite pick to win the tournament. Hands down it was assumed that Julia could hold her own against the best shots of the State Police, and would assuredly survive the early rounds and go on to compete against the winner during the final. All of the women, including Julia, were active members of the U.S.D.P.A., the United States Defensive Pistol Association. They practiced regularly, and were highly advanced in their small arms weaponry skills.

This morning's weather was sunny and refreshingly cool. Each of the competitors had brought along friends and family to watch the competition. Julia had already picked out a favorite restaurant venue for her and Reggie to enjoy a victory luncheon following the match, as she was that sure of her shooting skills. The shooting course was set up and would be judged by instructors of the U.S.D.P.A. and instructors from the V.S.P... The course was a variation on the V.S.P. 50 round Tactical Qualification for semiautomatic pistols. Each "combatant" would be allowed limited shots within a limited amount of seconds from different poses. The final round incorporated a make-shift hallway with doorframes on each side simulating actual rooms from which could spring cardboard silhouetted "bad guys," and "good guys" before the shooter reached the final target at the end of the hall. The objective was to keep cool and to not shoot any of the "good guy" figures. It was known as the "combat" round.

During the first round, the paired shooters from each team would, on command, draw and fire 6 rounds in 8 seconds from point shoulder positions. Next, on command, they would fire 4 rounds with their weak, non-preferred hand only, point shoulder position in 10 seconds. Both rounds were conducted with targets set at 7 yards away.

The second round was fired at a distance of 15 yards. On command, the competitors would draw their weapons and fire 2 rounds in 3 seconds; then re-holster and repeat for a total of 6 rounds. At the conclusion of this round, only the best scoring shooters remained for round three, and the runners-up competitors with lower scores were invited to join the observant bystanders. Not surprisingly, Julia Dolenz and Jared McClure were two of the four remaining shooters that would participate in this round. The Williamsburg Women's Team was feeling proud that in addition to Julia, another one of their teammates was shooting in round three.

Round three was the most difficult as the targets were set 25 yards away. On command, the shooter would approach a straw barricade, assume a kneeling position and then draw their weapon and fire 6 rounds. The next drill was to repeat the number of shots from a standing barricade position, until a total of 12 rounds have been fired within a 45 second window of time. Although each competitor turned in a great performance, when the round was over and the scoring verified, it would be Julia Dolenz against Jared McClure in the final, "combat" round.

As they walked over to the last part of the firing range, McClure spoke to Julia.

"You're one hell of a shot, Ms. Dolenz," McClure said. "I see that you shoot with a 9mm instead of a .22. They're heavier and have more recoil to handle. Again, impressive." He smiled. She looked up and him and returned the smile, but not the compliment.

"You mean, impressive...for a woman. Isn't that what you mean, Lt. McClure?"

"No ma'am," he said. "I apologize if that's what you thought that I meant. It's just that I know of a lot of guys who prefer a .22 when they're shooting, especially from 25 yards. You handle your weapon expertly. Congratulations on getting to the final round."

"Thank you," Julia said. "You were last year's champion, were you not?"

"Yes ma'am," he said.

"Would you have any advice for the upcoming, combat round that you'd be willing to share?"

He was quiet for a moment as he continued to walk. He looked ahead as they approached their destination.

"I'd be happy to offer you my wishes for good luck. Just stay cool and focused. You'll do fine. It's actually quite an adrenaline rush with one, huge bonus, win or draw."

"What's the bonus?" She said.

"The bad guys aren't shooting back at you," he said as he smiled.

"Oh," Julia said, as she was reminded of her safe, civilian status. "Quite right. Quite right."

Then they both reported to the judge's table where they would receive instructions for the final round. On a coin toss, it was decided that McClure would shoot first. Julia was lost somewhere inside herself concentrating on what she was about to observe. She hadn't wished "Good Luck" to Lt. McClure.

He noticed that, then put everything out of his mind except for the matter at hand. It was just like another day on the job, clearing a structure of possible suspects, with the exception that he had stated to Julia beforehand. He knew the cardboard figures were just those. Not living human beings. If he made a mistake, no one would be hurt. For him, this was a low stakes exercise. It was entertainment, exciting, and fun.

For Julia, who always struggled with her gargantuan ego, it was high stakes, and she was processing the upcoming task much differently than McClure. She always demanded perfection of herself no matter what task she threw herself into.

Her palms were sweating, and she had to dry them by rubbing them up and down the sides of her jeans as she studied McClure approaching the simulation. This was stressful, nerve-wracking, and trying.

His gun was holstered. On command, he would draw his weapon and he would have 60 seconds to get to the end of the "hallway," and then take a shot at the final target that was set at 7 yards away. He had 6 shots loaded into the magazine of his SIG Sauer P226 service pistol. He knew as he stood there, ready for the command from the judge, that if he misfired at even a single phantom made of cardboard that could emerge from behind any door in the hallway, he wouldn't have enough time to reload his weapon for the final target shot. He took in a long breath, gave his shoulders, arms, and hands a quick shake, and nodded towards the judge.

"Draw your weapon!" The judge barked. McClure obeyed and then got himself into some form of a cat-like crouch with the SIG Sauer held in front of him with both hands. The crowd of spectators standing behind at a safe distance could feel the tension in the air. The judge looked at his timer. "Go!" he said and he clicked the button. McClure was on a deadline that he ignored. He walked steadily on down the simulated hallway, using his peripheral vision to scan left and right. He passed two doors on the left and two on the right before a door opened on his left. A phantom cardboard silhouette quickly appeared and "stepped" into the hallway. Within a half-second, McClure shot the figure in the middle of the mass and stepped forward. The make- believe figure was a "bad guy." A white male wearing a gray hoodie holding out a .357 steel-plated Smith & Wesson. It was a righteous shoot on the part of McClure. The spectators applauded quietly.

Within another 5 seconds, another door on his left appeared. The figure looking like a young woman in jeans holding out a metallic object straight ahead at him in a shoulder point position. McClure ignored it and took another step. It was a good call. The young woman figure was holding out an old style flip phone. Next, two doors, one on each side of him opened and out popped two figures. He fired at the figure to his left and then fired to his right, hitting the figure in the left in the stomach and the figure on the right in the head.

They were both bad guy targets. The one on the left was wielding a Bowie knife, the one on the right had a sawed-off shotgun that he held at his hip. Again, perfect calls, and the impressed audience applauded.

He was almost to the end of the hall when a door on his right opened and a tall figure in a menacing pose popped out. It was the figure of a large white male in a torn t-shirt, much taller than McClure, with a scowl on his bleeding face and his arms raised above him in what appeared to be rage. The spectators gasped while McClure checked his weapon. The simulated subject, though menacing, was unarmed. Ten seconds left. In the last 50 seconds, five targets had been presented to McClure and his judgement was perfect.

He cleared the last of the hallway without any more make-believe intruders popping out at him. He assumed the standard police combat position: legs shoulder length apart, knees bent, weight slightly forward, weapon held in both hands as he fired at the last target.

It was a "kill" shot to the middle of the forehead of the cardboard target. The audience could now give him a loud round of applause. Among the spectators was an admiring Trooper Fred Drury together with another one of his police buddies, clapping enthusiastically.

McClure returned to the judge's table and looked over at Julia Dolenz. She nodded respectfully at him. The simulation was now being re-set with new targets that would emerge from different doors that had opened for McClure. The judge and timekeeper nodded in her direction and Julia stepped over to her mark at the start of the simulation.

"Draw your weapon!" The judge barked. Julia obeyed and stood straight with her Glock 19 held in her right hand dangling down her right leg. She loosened up her shoulders and looked straight ahead. The crowd of spectators standing behind at a safe distance could feel the tension building in the air once more. Reginald White looked on. He knew how important this was to Julia.

The judge looked at his timer. "Go!" he said, and he clicked the button. Like McClure, Julia now took on a crouch, with her weapon held out in front in her right hand. Within a few seconds of stepping into the hallway simulation, a door flung wide open to her right and a cardboard male figure emerged wearing a black leather vest over his bare chest and a red bandana around his forehead. Julia pumped two shots into the figure; one through his head and another through his chest where his heart would have been. She made a righteous shoot, as the phantom bad guy figure was holding an Uzi in his hand. The audience clapped respectfully as they had for McClure. Reggie was beaming a broad smile.

She passed a pair of doors to her left and another pair to her right when two doors opened simultaneously from either side. She shot the figure on the left twice and almost immediately with the same deadly pattern that she had delivered to the first cardboard figure. It was another bad guy in a tee-shirt brandishing a chain.

In another half-second, she shot the figure to her right. One bullet to the figure's head. The audience groaned softly behind her as she took a second closer look at her shooting "victim." It turned out to be a guy with a mustache holding up a paper sack of groceries between his two arms and he was holding out a black metal object in his hands as if he were pointing a pistol. But it wasn't a pistol. It was his car keys and his car alarm whose button he was pushing. She had "killed" a good guy.

"Fuck," she said.

She was halfway down the contrived hallway when another door flung open to her left. She pointed the Glock at the target then pulled it up and away. It was a good call. The simulated person was a tall African-American youth wearing shades and dressed in gang paraphernalia holding out a cell phone. Before she knew it, the last door on the right opened and another target emerged. In a half-second she shot the target once in the middle of the mass. It was a bad guy, ski mask covering the face, was pointing a sawed-off shotgun in her direction.

Aware of the precious seconds left in the simulation, she walked forward hastily, scanning the hallway left and right. She reached the end of the hall and found the last target. She aimed her weapon in a classic shoulder point pose at the cardboard target placed 7 yards away and squeezed the trigger on the Glock and heard the sickening sound of the firing pin striking cold metal. "Click." She was out of ammo. She released the clip with frenzied speed and started to reload when she heard the judge call out, "Time! Holster your weapon, please."

Her heart sank. She was no rookie to simulations such as this and yet, she made the simplest of rookie mistakes in not keeping track of her shots. She had been limited by the rules to 6 shots, just as McClure. Where he had the discipline to fire one shot at each of the targets, Julia had been firing off two at several of the targets and not paying attention. She had also "shot" a civilian. She turned back to report to the judge's table intent to swallow her pride and to congratulate Lt. McClure on his repeat champion performance. She held out her right hand as she closed the distance with McClure.

"Congratulations, Lt. McClure," Julia said. "Your performance was brilliant."

McClure shook her hand.

"Congratulations to you, too, Ms. Dolenz. If I were a bad guy, I would not want to run into you in a dark alley. You're a superb shot, and you handled yourself well. It's been a privilege to shoot with you today. If I can be of any assistance to you in the future, please let me know." He handed her his police business card.

She looked at the card and looked up at him and smiled. They both walked over to a small podium where McClure and Julia took their places together with the two runners-up finalists, one from the V.S.P. and the other from the Williamsburg women's club. McClure was awarded the large, engraved "First Place" trophy. Julia of course received a smaller trophy marked "Second Place," and the others received smaller statuettes labeled "Runners-Up."

Julia congratulated her team mate and re-joined Reggie, who had promised her a first-rate lunch despite coming in second place. The crowd thinned, and Fred Drury stopped by to congratulate Jared McClure.

"That was an even more impressive performance than last year's, sir. Congratulations!" He held out his hand and McClure shook it.

"Thanks, Fred," he said as he looked yards away at a departing Julia and company.

"You had some stiff competition with that Mrs. Dolenz, I must say," Drury said.

"That's for sure," McClure said as he continued to stare after her.

McClure looked back at Drury.

"Again, congratulations, sir." Drury said.

"Me and a couple of the guys and gals from the Luray office would like to take you out for a beer."

"Are you guys buying?" McClure said with a smile.

"That's affirmative, sir. Considering how much money we all took from some of the guys at the other posts who bet against you."

McClure laughed.

"Well then," he said. "Then I'd be a fool not to come along, provided one thing?"

"Sure," Drury said.

"Stop calling me, 'sir'."

Drury nodded and they turned and walked towards the parking lot.

Chapter 10

Another morning was dawning in Duck. Paul and Megan Treadwell, together with their dog Brandy, were taking a walk south from their oceanside home on Spyglass Road towards the Army Research Pier. They both enjoyed seeing the first rays of sunlight break over the dark horizon and watched as the sun changed the color of the sky from black to a mix of purple and red before it turned blue. There were a few wisps of clouds in this morning's sky and already squadrons of pelicans were skimming the crests of the incoming waves scanning for schooling fish.

"I'll never get tired of this," Megan said as she unclipped Brandy's leash. Paul tossed a tennis ball towards the surf and off she went to retrieve it.

"Me neither," Paul said.

"Remember how concerned I was when we lived back in Ohio that Brandy would never adapt to ocean living?" Megan said.

"Yep." Paul said. "And that concern went away on the first trip that we took with her on vacation years ago when she was a pup. Now I couldn't imagine her being happy without the ocean at her front door."

Soaking wet, Brandy returned and dropped the tennis ball at Paul's feet.

"Did you see in the paper this morning that the developers have been given the OK to build that big water park on the causeway just over the bridge on the mainland?" Megan said. Paul bent down and grabbed the ball and tossed it again. Brandy woofed and chased after it.

"Yes I did. We both kinda' figured it would happen. Better on the mainland than here, is what I say. All this development is putting too much pressure on these barrier islands. They were never intended to be so populous year- round. You and I have seen it build up over the years. It's great for our restaurant business, but I am concerned about how much more development and traffic the Banks can handle during tourist season."

"Me too," Megan said. "I'd hate to see the very beauty of this place that attracted us here in the first place destroyed by over-development. And you *know* that I worry about the horses."

Paul nodded. Brandy was ahead of them sniffing and digging up the sand, curious about something along the surf line.

Megan was referring to the last herd of wild Spanish Mustangs that roamed the northern beaches in Corolla and beaches north of there such as Carova. They were descended from a herd that was brought to the New World in the 16th century. With each passing year there was less land for the herd to find food and flourish, and they were still in danger of being struck by vehicles. Paul and Megan contributed handsomely each year to the Corolla Wild Horse Fund.

"Kim still coming over for a private breakfast this morning?" Paul said.

"Yes," Megan said. "She's anxious to give me some news. Probably about one of the guys she's seeing." Paul nodded and studied Brandy who had moved on down the beach. They were almost to the pier.

"Guess we'd better turn around and get back then," Paul said. "I'd like to give Gunny some help in the kitchen before the staff arrives. Kim does know that we're not open for breakfast?"

"She does know. I told her that she would be helping us sample a new quiche that Gunny is whipping up this morning. You know? Sort of a taste test."

Paul looked at her and frowned.

"Gunny has made our restaurant the most highly-rated on the Outer Banks. He doesn't need taste testers especially if he's personally preparing something."

Megan cocked her head and looked up at her husband.

"No shit, Sherlock, and Mr. Former detective," she said. "I just told Kim that so she didn't feel as if she'd be mooching off of our good nature."

"Oh," Paul said. "Okay."

Within ninety minutes Megan and Paul were back at The Brown Pelican located a short distance from where they lived.

"Good morning, Gunny," they called out in unison as they approached the bar.

"Hey, you two," Books called out from the kitchen. "I'll be out in a few minutes."

"Take your time," Paul said.

The restaurant had the look of coastal casual chic. The floors were white and black checkerboard. The walls were trimmed in attractive wood. Bottles of different colors stood atop glass shelving behind the wooden bar. The colors were neutral with the exception of the red leather bar stools that had seats as well as backs, trimmed in chrome, giving them a funky 1950's diner look.

A half hour later, Kim arrived and she and Megan grabbed an open table that looked out over the Currituck Sound. Books had set up the table settings and had placed a fresh flower arrangement in the center. Just outside the window where they sat the shallow waters of the Currituck Sound stretched out before them. It appeared quite blue today reflecting the nearly cloud-free sky. Out on the water close up they could see people paddle boarding and farther out, the more adventurous tourists were para-sailing. They were each enjoying a mimosa when Gunny Books approached the table and set down two plates that held slices of his latest quiche together with slices of strawberries and melons.

"Spinach, Tomato and Feta Quiche," Books said with a smile. "Bon appetit," he said before he turned and walked back to the bar to go over today's menu with Paul.

"This looks divine," Kim said, pointing down at the quiche with her fork. Megan and Kim both took their first bites of quiche.

Megan nodded. "We're spoiled around here. Frederick Douglass Books is the best head chef on the Outer Banks. He wins every Taste of The Beach cooking competition down here."

"Paul's no slouch as a bartender, either. This mimosa is fantastic. Thanks for the treat, friend."

"My pleasure," Megan said. "Let's dig in." They both had several bites of food, and their consensus was that it was the best quiche either one of them had ever eaten.

"So," Megan said. "How are things going with David? It *is* David, isn't it?"

Kim shook her head and stopped chewing.

"There *was* a David. I dumped the weirdo soon after we last had lunch together."

"Okay," Megan said as she took another bite of quiche and looked back out at the Sound.

"That's all you're going to say?"

"I figure if it's none of my business you'll tell me so, and if you want to talk about it that you'll get to it eventually, that's all." Megan returned her gaze towards her friend.

"He took me out to dinner and *proposed*," Kim said.

"That does sound weird. I didn't think that you guys were that serious yet."

"We *weren't* that serious yet. At least I wasn't. I told you a couple of weeks ago that I found certain things odd about him? Well, he had even brought an engagement ring to dinner that night. It was a big, bad-ass diamond ring. Can you believe it?"

Megan shrugged.

"What exactly did he say?" Megan said. "I mean, what made him think that marriage was in the cards for the two of you so early on in your... relationship?"

Kim finished her quiche and put down her fork. She tented her long fingers and tapped her chin.

"I haven't a clue what he was thinking. We weren't even sleeping with one another. He said that we were destined by the stars to be together forever, or something like that. It really creeped me out! I mean, I knew nothing much about this guy other than the few things he told me about himself."

"That does sound creepy. So... What did you say to him?"

"I told him no, of course. I told him that I didn't really know him; that he always seemed so secretive about stuff. I told him that his proposal was a complete shock to me, and I also told him that I had met someone else, and that I had no interest in seeing him again."

"You were just making up the part about there being a new guy to blow him off, right?"

"No. Seriously. I'll tell you all about him. He's marvelous."

"Okay," Megan said. "So how did David take your rejection? You did say that you dumped him."

"That's another odd thing about this guy. He took it rather well, I thought. He asked a few questions about my new guy friend – which I didn't answer – and he put the ring back in his jacket and said, 'Very well then. No hard feelings. Best of luck.' You know? That sort of thing. Then we finished dinner, and I got an Uber driver to take me back home. I didn't want to get into David's car."

Megan studied her friend for a moment as she too finished the last bite of quiche on her plate. She took a slow pull on her mimosa. Kim did the same.

"So have you heard from him since?" Megan said.

"No, thankfully. I cancelled my account on that website where I had found him and deleted any photos that I had of him on my phone. What a very strange man he was. I also sensed that there was a dark side of him that luckily I didn't get to see... Oh well. Happily, life goes on."

"Where did you find the new guy?" Megan asked.

"On Facebook," Kim said smiling.

Megan shook her head and grabbed her glass and drained her mimosa. She looked over towards the bar.

"Oh *Barkeeper*?" She said in a loud voice. "Two more of these on the double, please." She held up the empty long stemmed glass in her hand.

"Coming right up," Paul shouted back.

"Chef Books!" Kim said in a loud, clear voice. "This is the best quiche that I have ever enjoyed in my life. Thank you!"

Gunny turned in his stool towards her and smiled.

"You're welcome Miss Kim." He turned back to watch Paul prepare two more drinks. When Paul finished, he brought them over to his wife and her friend, bussed the table and returned to his discussion with Gunny.

"You found the new guy on Facebook," Megan said. "Of course you did. What's *this* guy's name if you don't mind me asking?"

"I don't mind. You and Paul and Mr. Books are going to meet him soon enough. I'm making a reservation to have dinner here with him as soon as you can find an open night. His name is Chip Walker. He's a great guy, Megan. He never married. He loves the outdoors.

Hang gliding, water sailing, surfing, stargazing. We like the same music and foods. He's the owner of the hang gliding school at Jockey's Ridge. He's already taken me up for a couple of tandem rides over the dunes. It's thrilling." Kim took a sip of her new drink. "Chip is the guy that I'm going to marry someday. And soon, I think."

"Wow!" Megan said. "You're that sure already?"

"Yes," Kim said and nodded. "How soon did you know in your heart of hearts that you were going to marry Paul?"

"It only took a couple of dates before I started thinking about it," Megan said as she took another sip of her drink.

"Then you know what I'm talking about," Kim said as she and Megan both looked back at the bar to Paul.

"Yes I do," Megan said as she held up her glass in the form of a toast. Kim did likewise as they clinked glasses.

"Congratulations, girlfriend," Megan said.

"Thanks Megan," Kim said.

"One last question?" Megan said.

"Shoot."

"How old is he?"

"Five years older than me."

"Even better," Megan said with a smile.

The screen door entrance squeaked, and in walked Marty Tate in full uniform.

"Mornin' everybody," Tate said in a loud, friendly greeting.

"Hey Marty!" Everyone, with the exception of Kim, said back. Kim had yet to meet the Treadwell's chief law enforcement friend.

"Coffee on?" Tate asked.

"It sure is," Paul said from behind the bar. "Come on in."

Tate first walked over towards Megan who stood up and gave Tate a hug.

"Marty, I want you to meet my friend, Kim Montgomery," Megan said. Kim stood up and shook Tate's hand.

"A pleasure to meet you, Sheriff," Kim said.

"The pleasure is all mine," Tate said. "Tell me, what are you two pretty ladies doing in the company of those ugly bums sitting over there?" Tate jerked his head towards the bar and grinned. Megan and Kim chuckled.

"Why don't y' all step over here bawse Marty, and that way *all* the ugliness be on *this* side of the room?" Books said in his best field-hand, stepin fetchit impression.

"Excuse me ladies," Tate said as he nodded his head. "I need to speak with Mutt and Jeff for a few minutes."

Tate walked over and took a seat at the bar next to Books as Paul set a cup of coffee down in front of him.

Chapter 11

"So, what brings you to the far reaches of Dare County this morning?" Paul said from behind the bar.

Sanderling, just north of Duck, is the last community incorporated into Dare County. Corolla and the northern - most beaches of the Outer Banks are a part of Currituck County, and under the jurisdiction of Sheriff Frank Meekins.

"I was asked to make a presentation to the Duck Town Council," Tate said before he took a pull on his coffee mug.

"Impressive," Books said with a grin on his face. "Like a real stand up presentation with PowerPoint slides and maybe even using a remote control?"

Tate smiled back at him.

"As a matter of fact, yes Gunny. With a real remote control and all."

"You must really be looking forward to that," Paul said.

"As much as I'd be looking forward to root canal surgery," Tate said. "Actually, it won't take that long. It's just a review of emergency preparedness measures now that we're back in tourist season, and with the annual Fourth of July parade coming up."

"Megan and I were at the Town Hall last night as a matter of fact," Paul said. "We volunteered this year to serve on the planning commission for the parade. Last night we selected the Grand Marshalls."

"I must admit that 'Lizbeth and I had a little fun as the Grand Marshalls last year," Tate said. "So, who gets the honors this year?"

"Yeah," Books said. "You haven't even mentioned that to me yet this morning. Do tell."

Paul took a swig from his coffee mug, then jerked his head in the direction of the front door of the restaurant.

"Our next door neighbor and her husband. Mrs. Mary Kay Cullipher."

Mrs. Cullipher – or Mrs. 'C' as she sometimes referred to herself – was the owner and operator of the general store located next to the restaurant. She had named the place Duck Dry Goods: Quacks-R-Us-Everything Ducky. Thanks to her business savvy, the successful shop has been in business for over twenty five years, and Paul and Megan and Books were all fond of Mrs. C.

"Our local town gossip and her husband are going to be the parade grand marshals?" Book said. "She be tickled."

"Nice choice," Tate said. "The 4th is coming up fast. When are you going to tell her?"

"Another member of the planning commission will tell her soon. It'll feel more official to her that way." Paul said. "And Gunny's right. She'll be thrilled. She deserves it."

Paul studied Tate for a few more seconds. The two of them had become close friends after they and Books had rescued Megan from the hands of a terrifying killer last August. Paul could tell that Tate had something on his mind besides a presentation.

"How's your homicide investigation going?" Paul said.

Tate pursed his lips, looked down at the bar, and shook his head a little before he answered.

"Let's just say that I'm missing a few things," he said as he looked back up at Paul.

"Like what?" Gunny asked.

"A weapon. Fingerprints. DNA. Witnesses. Hair and fiber evidence. A suspect."

"Oh," both Paul and Gunny chimed in together. "Those things," Paul said.

"Yeah," Tate said. "The case is getting colder by the day."

"Didn't you tell us that a colleague of yours in Virginia is working on a similar case?" Paul said.

"Not similar. Connected." Tate said. "Lt. Jared McClure of the Virginia State Police, and he's got less than me. All he's got is the photographs of a dead body that was found in the Shenandoah National Park and some interview notes that were taken when it was a missing person's case a year ago."

"And you both are sure that it's the same guy who did both murders?" Gunny said.

"Yep. Same small caliber gun used, both shot in the face, and both men missing their wedding ring fingers post mortem. Last year he did the deed in Virginia. Now here, a couple of weeks ago."

"Sounds like one sick sonovabitch," Gunny said as he shook his head.

"Any indication of motive?" Paul asked. "Greed? Anger? Jealousy? Money? Revenge? With both victims shot in the face, it sounds as if it could be rage or revenge, and it doesn't sound as if a woman did the crimes."

Tate shrugged his shoulders.

"That's the direction of where we're leaning, but we really don't know. Could be any or all of the five you mentioned. Both victims were well- liked. Both had money. Both of them were engaged to be married. Neither one of them had any enemies that we can locate, but, someone hated them both enough to kill them and maim them afterwards."

"How long had these victims been engaged before the mystery guy aced them within a year of one another?"

Tate looked up at Paul again, knitted thick eyebrows and made a face.

"I don't remember exactly, but, it's in the notes for sure. Why do you ask, Treadwell?"

"If you've already turned the victims' lives inside out, another avenue of inquiry might lie in the past of the women that these two men were engaged to."

Tate nodded.

"The Charlottesville police interviewed the grieving fiancé' in Virginia last year, and Kenny and I interviewed the woman here recently."

"But did you dig deep enough into their *past* boyfriends? The ones that they had *before* they got engaged to their dead fiancés? One of them might turn out to be a past lover scorned."

Tate rubbed his thick mustache with his right hand as he considered this.

"Sounds like you might be on to something," Books said to Paul.

"As I said, Kenny and I interviewed our latest victim's fiancé' about that but not thoroughly," Tate said. "Tell me where you're going with this Paul. Let's stay focused on my homicide investigation here. Are you saying that the woman that we interviewed here on the Outer Banks dated some guy in her past that could turn out to be a jealous former lover?"

Paul nodded.

"And maybe she dumped this guy before she met the true love of her life in Dr. McCleney."

"Keep going," Paul said as he rolled his right hand in a circular gesture.

"And this same guy got enraged enough to kill the new man that showed up later in her life? That sounds like we'd be stretching the laws of probabilities to their limits. Besides, if he's that big of a whack job, wouldn't it make more sense that he'd be trying to harm the woman that dumped him instead of the good doctor?"

"Maybe. But consider this. Maybe this mystery guy didn't kill new men who showed up later in her life," Paul said. "But the new man that she became *engaged* to. The man that she was going to *marry*. The wedding ring finger is the killer's signature. This individual could turn out to be some highly over- jealous sociopath who rages against his own humiliation or rejection. He's patient and calculating. He wants to teach what he most likely calls her - a bitch - he wants to teach 'the bitch' a lesson. He's reasoning that, 'If I'm not good enough for you, then nobody is going to be' or some bat - shit crazy thing like that. He shot the victim in the face which suggests he viewed this killing as an execution, permanently eliminating his rival. Who knows?" Paul threw his arms in the air and then grabbed his coffee cup.

Tate looked over at Books who was listening intently to Paul's hunch. He pointed up at Paul with his right hand.

"You know, Gunny. Treadwell really has a twisted mind, doesn't he?"

"And you're just figuring that out now?" Gunny said with a smile. They both looked back at Paul who hiked his shoulders.

"I can't help it. It's that FBI profiler training that you and I both got up in Quantico years back, Marty. You were tops in your class. So that must make you at least as twisted as me."

"True," Tate said. "And you were the top of your class. Seriously, you might be on to something, Paul. It's a fresh line of inquiry, that's for sure. It also suggests that this guy would have been stalking the woman here for a time after she split up with him. As you suggest he's not interested in men that she may have been casually dating. He'd have to find evidence that she had become engaged. Maybe a newspaper announcement or social media."

Chapter 12

The next late June morning found Kenny Smith and Marty Tate back at the home of Anne Scarborough, situated in the sea and sound side community of Southern Shores. Southern Shores was a well-established community of the Northern Banks and was planned and built originally during the 1950's by Frank Stick. Stick was an artist, a real estate developer, and a conservationist who helped erect the first sand dunes supplanted with sea grass to stave off beach erosion. His son, David, would become an acclaimed historian of the region.

Tate and Smith were seated opposite Ms. Scarborough who was an attractive blond in her early thirties. She stood just under six feet tall with a curvaceous figure, and captivating green eyes. She had on a pale blue cotton top which draped over the top of her jeans. Both Tate and Smith noticed that she no longer wore the engagement ring that had been given to her by the late Dr. McCleney. They were each having coffee that she had ready for them upon their arrival. After some small talk about tourist season traffic they turned to the main reason for their visit.

"Sheriff Tate and Officer Smith, I am glad that you're still on the case. Can you tell me if you have any fresh leads about the person who killed Phillip?" Anne said.

Tate chose not to disclose the parallel case on the Virginia mainland.

"We've studied the surveillance video footage from the marina and it revealed nothing, which may suggest that the intruder was familiar with the camera placements and was careful with his movements. We believe that he had been there before and had planned his attack on Dr. McCleney carefully. He left no trace evidence behind except for a spent shell casing."

"So, you're certain that you're looking for a man then?" Anne interrupted.

"Yes," Tate said. He continued.

"We now also know the probable make and model of the weapon that was used. We canvassed all the other boat owners throughout the marina and no one saw anything unusual that night."

"Unusual?" Anne asked.

"Yes," Kenny Smith said. "Such as a muzzle flash from the weapon, or seeing anyone there that night that they hadn't seen before. Any vehicles that they hadn't seen before. Those sorts of things."

"I see," Anne said.

"We're chasing down all additional leads as we get them," Tate said in an effort to assuage any doubts that she might have about forward progress with the investigation. "And, that's why we're here this morning. There are some questions that Kenny and I did not ask during your first interview that we would like to ask now, if that's alright with you?"

"Of course," Anne said. "I'll help in any way that I can but I think I told you everything about Philip and me that you wanted to know."

"You have," Tate said. "The questions that I have this morning are more about your past. Your past before you met Phillip."

"I don't understand," Anne said with a tincture of confusion and apprehension in her voice. "I thought you said that your suspect is an unknown male."

"Please try to relax, Ms. Scarborough," Kenny Smith said. "You're in no way a suspect in this case. You never were." He looked over at Tate as if he were seeking some form of permission. Tate nodded as if he could read his mind. Smith continued.

"You see... Phillip's wedding ring finger was missing from his body at the crime scene."

Anne Scarborough's right hand came rushing up to her chin. Her face turned red.

"What?! Are you telling me that...? Someone *cut* Phillips' finger *off* of his hand?!"

"Yes, ma'am," Smith said. "But after he was dead."

"But he wasn't tortured then killed?" She shrieked.

"No, Ms. Scarborough," Tate interjected. "The coroner's office confirmed that this brutal act was done postmortem. His unfortunate end was quick and painless. I know that's of no consolation. We're sorry to be giving you this additional detail. You'll remember that the funeral director felt it best that Phillip had a closed casket memorial service. When you viewed his body his left hand was covered by a sheet. That's why you didn't know. That, and we chose *not* to release this information until now. Now, only those of us conducting the investigation, yourself, and the killer obviously, know this. We're sorry. It's a detail that was never given to the press and it will never be disclosed." His voice was strong and measured and confident. Anne nodded her head and wiped away a few tears with a paper napkin.

"I too am again sorry for your loss, Ms. Scarborough," Kenny said. "It's just that Sheriff Tate and I both felt that if you didn't know this detail that you wouldn't understand our line of questioning. You see, as Sheriff Tate said, we'd like to talk awhile about your past before you met Phillip and got engaged to him. We wanted to find out about men that you may have dated before you met Phillip. If that's okay?"

"It is," she said. "But I need a glass of water." She stood up and hurried over to the kitchen sink. Tate and Smith were silent during the break in the discussion. When she returned to the dining room table, the color of her skin appeared normal.

"Sorry," she said. "That was a lot to take in a minute ago."
Tate and Smith both nodded.
"Of course," Tate said. "Are you alright to continue?"
She nodded.
"Go ahead with your questions."
Tate looked over at Smith who pulled out his notepad.
"Tell us again how and where you and Phillip first met?" Smith said.

"As I believe that I told you before. We met through a website dedicated to helping couples find lasting, long term relationships. It's called *Happily-Ever-After.com*."

"Do you have to subscribe to the service?" Tate asked.
"Yes," Anne said. "They have a thorough on-line vetting process before you submit your personal information."

"Do you still subscribe to the service?" Kenny asked.
Anne shook her head. "No. Phillip was the second failed relationship that came as a result of that website. I now consider it bad luck to be a member."

Tate and Smith exchanged glances before Tate eased out another question.

"We'd like to pry a bit into that other relationship, if that's okay? What you tell us about this other individual - anything at all - could be helpful in our investigation."

Anne wrapped her long arms around herself and leaned into the table.

"The other man's name was David. I was introduced to him via the website about five to six months before I met Phillip."

"What is his last name?" Kenny asked as he paused taking notes.

"Wiggins. David Wiggins. He was – is, I guess – young and good looking. Charming as charming can be at first, but secretive and spooky. I honestly don't know how he cleared the vetting process on the website. I didn't think that he was normal."

"Go on, please. Tell us all that you can remember about him," Tate said.

"Our relationship lasted shy of two months. He told me that he was a venture capitalist by trade. I still don't know much about that, but, he always had money and he paid with cash for everything. Our meals. Our entertainment. Even gasoline for his car. I mean, who does that these days in a paperless society? He used to spend a lot of time talking to me about what he considered to be the perfect woman and the perfect wife, and then one day, he started calling me those things!

We hadn't even slept together and he's calling me his destiny child or some bullshit like that. Excuse my French, guys, but I think that he was seriously fucked in his head." She tapped her left temple with her left hand to emphasize her point.

Tate nodded and Smith continued to take notes.

"So, tell us about the breakup," Tate said. "I assume that you were the one to end the relationship?"

Anne nodded vigorously.

"Oh, you *bet* I did. He took me out to dinner one night and proposed! He even brought along a ring for the occasion. It freaked me out. I told him that I didn't see that coming. That I was feeling rushed and quite confused. I told him, 'no,' and that I felt it would be better not to see him again."

"And how did he take the news?" Kenny asked in a calm tone, without revealing his enthusiasm for the intelligence that he and Tate were obtaining.

"Here's another freaky thing about this guy," she said. "Of all the men that I've dated in the past, he took it well. Very well, in fact. He put the ring back in the box and asked if my final word was 'no'. When I nodded he said something like, 'Very well then my dear. No hard feelings. There are a lot of other fish in the sea. I won't be troubling you further; best of luck,' and then he stood up and left the restaurant. True to his word, I've never heard from him or seen him since. I've had my share of men who wouldn't take 'no' for an answer, but this guy was easy to let go."

"Forgive me for my next question," Tate said. "Do you think that David would be capable of harming Phillip, assuming that he heard or saw someplace that you were going to be married?"

Anne sat with a look of astonishment sweeping over her face at Tate's suggestion.

"No," she said with what sounded like confidence to the two men. She shook her head. "No. I couldn't bring myself to believe that. Have you ever heard of anything like what you're suggesting, Sheriff?"

Tate let out an audible breath of air from his nose and pursed his lips.

"Yes," he said. "I'm afraid so. The classic jilted lover. The way that Dr. McCleney was killed suggests that his killer was in a rage. The missing wedding ring finger is strongly suggestive. We call it the killer's signature. Mr. Wiggins may have presented himself as a non-violent person to you, but, it would not be the first time that a killer was described as 'charming.'"

"Like Ted Bundy?" she said.

"Exactly," Tate said, surprised at her age that she would remember one of the worst predators put to death for the trail of dead women that he left behind during his killing spree decades ago.

"Did you and Phillip make a public announcement about your engagement?" Kenny asked.

"Yes we did," she said. "We made an announcement in *The Coastland Waves* newspaper, and we both posted the news to our friends on our Facebook pages."

Kenny took note of what she said.

"David could have seen that announcement in the paper. Is that what you're saying?"

"It's possible," Tate said. "If he were still here in the Outer Banks. There are people who can easily hack into Facebook accounts as well, I'm afraid."

"I didn't realize that," she said.

"Facebook doesn't like to admit it, I'm afraid," Kenny said.

"Where did David live?" Tate asked.

"That was another odd thing. He claimed that he rented a cottage in Duck, but, I never saw the inside of it. Wait a minute," Anne said as she smacked her right hand on her forehead. "One day we stopped for gas in Duck at the station near Wee Winks."

"We know the place," Tate said. "What kind of car did he drive?"

"A white BMW. Anyway, David reached for his wallet and pulled out some cash, then tossed the wallet on to the center console. I couldn't help but look to see his photo on a Virginia driver's license."

"You're positive of this?" Tate said.

"Oh yes," she said. "It said 'David Wiggins' and had his photo but I couldn't read his address in Virginia before he came back to the car. Sorry."

"O.K.," Tate said. "Do you remember what *kind* of BMW he drove? The model number? Was it a convertible? Hardtop? Two-door? Four-door?"

"I'm really not sure of the model. I'm not that familiar with German cars. It was a sedan and it had four doors."

"That's okay. Would you remember the state license plates that were on the car?"

"They were Virginia plates. The state name is on the top of the plate instead of the bottom like North Carolina. I don't remember the plate number. It wasn't one of those vanity plates though."

"So, a white BMW with Virginia license plates," Kenny said as he made a note. "Do you have any pictures of this guy? What does he look like?"

"No," she said. "I got rid of them all. He's as tall as me. No facial hair. Brown hair kept neat and trimmed. He had spectacular blue eyes."

"That's fine," Tate said. "Would you be alright if you came down to our headquarters and allow a sketch artist draw a picture of what he looked like?"

"You're starting to scare me Sheriff, but yes if you think that's important."

Tate held out his big right hand and patted her on the shoulder.

"I don't mean to frighten you, Anne. This could be a real long shot. It may come to nothing, but everything is important in a murder investigation. Is there anything else? I don't suppose that you'd still have his phone number?"

She shook her head.

"Is there any other detail that you can remember about him?"

"You know, I don't know why I didn't mention this to you at the beginning. He had an English accent."

"You mean, as in British accent?" Kenny said.

"Yes. It was subtle. He could even turn it on and off, but it was clearly detectable. When I asked him about that he said that it was because he was born just outside of London. When I pressed him more about that and his family and his upbringing, he'd always change the topic. That's part of what I meant about him being secretive."

Tate stood up and Kenny followed suit. Anne stood as well and walked back to the kitchen and took a cell phone out of her purse and came back.

"I just remembered something," she said. "I don't know if it's important or not, but David gave me this phone." She held it out to Marty who took it in his hands and studied it.

"I suggest that you either get rid of this or at a minimum get the phone number changed," he said as he handed her back the phone.

"I did change the number some days after Phillip died," she said.

"Good," he said.

"Where do we go from here?" She asked.

"We'll go back to the cop shop and get our guy who is good with cyber forensics to investigate the Happily-Ever-After website. Mr. Wiggins may still have an account there and even if he deleted it we can get a court order to go after it. You'll have a sitting with our sketch artist as soon as you can. We'll contact the Virginia State Police and share the intelligence."

She smiled back at him.

78

"You sound like you're a thorough man, Sheriff."

"Believe me," Kenny said. "He is." He smiled back at her.

"Sheriff, what do you think are your prospects for finding out who did this to Phillip? I watched on TV somewhere that if the police don't get anything within the first 48 hours that it cuts the chances of finding the murderer by at least fifty percent."

"You're well-informed, Anne." Tate said. "But, it's my experience that these guys always make mistakes. We had a guy that we caught here last year who made the mistake of calling my office to taunt me about how he was a criminal genius and that we were just a bunch of dumb Southern shit kickers. During that call he revealed what turned out to be a vital lead that caught up to him in the end."

"Was he a murderer?" She asked.

"Yes," Tate said. "We kept it as low key as we could in the newspaper, but, the story eventually got out."

"I read that story, but, I didn't know that he called your office," she said.

"Please keep what we've told you here this morning confidential. Keep the faith and be careful about what you post on social media."

"Yes, I will. I can drive down later this afternoon. Thank you, Sheriff Tate. I guess that we'll be in touch?"

"Most certainly," he said.

"For what it's worth, I really don't think that David had anything to do with Phillip's death. As I've told you, he showed no outward signs of jealousy or anger when I turned down his marriage proposal. He hasn't been harassing me."

"I understand. When we locate him we'll talk to him and if he has a solid alibi about the night in question he'll be in the clear." Tate said. "But, given what you've told us this morning, we're at least obliged to find him and at the very least eliminate him as a possible suspect. There's no other male that you dated for more than several weeks during this past year or two?"

"No. Just casual dates. I'm confessing that I was putting a lot of faith in that website in order to find me someone special," she said as her voice trailed off.

"You did find someone special," Tate said. "Everyone we've talked to spoke very highly of Phillip. He was a good man and he didn't deserve this. Rest assured that this is an active investigation and we're investing resources all available resources. We'll keep you posted. Thank you for all of your time this morning."

She nodded and then showed them out.

Chapter 13

That same day the sun was shining brightly on the sandy dunes of Jockey's Ridge. Jockey's Ridge State Park is located at Mile Post 12 in Nags Head. It is the home of the tallest living sand dune along the East coast affording the visitor who climbs to the top views of both the Atlantic Ocean to the east and Roanoke Sound to the west. Nags Head is close to the location in Kill Devil Hills where the Wright Brothers made their historic heavier- than- air powered flights in 1903. Neighboring Kitty Hawk is a sea side community where the brothers Wilbur and Orville dined and slept during the days and nights that they visited the Outer Banks from Dayton, Ohio, while they conducted their earlier glider experiments. But, unlike what a lot of people are told, they never flew in Kitty Hawk. They flew and mastered their flying skills in Nags Head where today year- round winds of often 10-15 mph make Jockey's Ridge ideal for hang gliding.

Through a special arrangement with the State Park Service, Nags Head Hang Gliding School has been in successful operation for over 20 years. There, in an air- conditioned training room a handsome first- time novice to the sport was seated next to a very attractive and scantily- clad brunette of the opposite sex while two other male students looking to be in their twenties were receiving orientation and ground school instruction from Chip Walker, the owner of the school. The novice estimated Walker to be ten years older than he and taller. *Probably 6', 3"* he thought to himself. Walker also appeared to be athletic and light on his feet. He had pronounced and developed upper arm and shoulder muscles. He had brown hair with noticeable red highlights and brown eyes.

While the other two men appeared bored, the very attractive brunette sitting next to him in cut-off jeans and a blue bikini string halter top seemed to be falling on every one of the words that left Chip Walker's mouth.

"I wonder what the ladies see in him?" The novice whispered to her as he nudged her smooth skin gently with his elbow. He was careful, just as he had practiced, to isolate the specific sound of the letter, 'R' when he said the word 'wonder' just like anyone with an

American accent would. She turned and looked up to study him before she answered.

"Like, dude," she said. "He's so tall and handsome, and like, he's a great talker and totally successful. Like... What's not to like? He's like total eye candy, dude." She made a 'what-don't-you-get' gesture with her hands palms up and she hiked her shoulders before her adoring gaze returned to Chip Walker.

While the novice regarded her to be totally delicious and quite the eye candy herself, her use of the word 'like' five times in her short answer as a discourse marker annoyed him. "Valley Girl" would be his silent nickname for her.

"So, to summarize the last point," Chip Walker said to the small group. "You're going to have to get yourself used to running down a steep slope without looking down the hill. Once you get to that perfect speed the wing will be directing you forward instead of downward and you'll need to be looking out in order to steer properly. I hope that makes sense? What questions do you have?"

One of the males sitting on the other side of the room raised his hand.

"What if we freeze up while we're running to get takeoff speed?" He asked.

"That's a good question. You'll have an instructor with you the whole time to coach you through the takeoff. But, to answer your question, if you were to hesitate, the glider will obey the laws of gravity and it will get in front of you, and you'll likely lose your balance and fall."

Everyone in the small group nodded.

The Valley Girl raised her hand and asked a question.

"Chip... How fast do we have to run to get, like...airborne?"

Walker smiled at her.

"Another good question. Actually on most days due to the constant winds, all it takes is a steady jog. The Wright Brothers appreciated that and that's why they practiced here."

"Who are the Wright Brothers?" Valley Girl asked. Everyone in the small class turned to look at her in astonishment. Chip Walker took her apparent ignorance in stride.

"The fathers of aviation. The inventors of the airplane. Their monument and a great museum are close by. I'd recommend visiting them."

The girl nodded vigorously and smiled back at Chip.

Jeee....sus. The novice thought to himself silently. *Cute, but as dumb as a bloody fucking sack of hammers.*

"So, before we get you outside to one of our expert instructors, I'd like to show you a training video that will give you a visual benefit to everything that we've covered this morning," Walker said as he dimmed the lights and played the video.

Once outside, the four new students were assigned a coach and a glider and they were off for their five flights over the sandy dunes. The novice male who had been seated next to the attractive brunette during the ground school session volunteered to fly first. The coach helped him into the harness and helped him launch for a flight that lifted him ten feet off of the sand and carried him a distance of almost one hundred yards. It felt exhilarating as his white glider with the three blue stripes soared in concert with other gliders and dozens and dozens of multi - colored kites of all kinds and varieties. The vast Atlantic Ocean stretched out in the distance before him and he banked the glider south parallel with the highway and he came to a soft landing. He crash landed only once, which for a novice he was told, was impressive.

Two hours later he was back inside the gift shop of the school which catered to the sport and stocked T-shirts as well as high tech, single, dual, and quad line kites of all different colors and patterns. He selected a souvenir T-shirt for himself and went to the cash register and pulled out a small, neat wad of cash and paid for it. As he was heading for the door, Chip Walker waved his hand over his head and got his attention. He headed over towards him.

"So," Chip said. "How did it go out there for you today?"

Resisting his instinctive impulse to say that it was "smashing," he replied.

"It was totally awesome," he said, sounding like one of today's air-headed teenagers that he despised.

"Great! Good to hear!" Chip said. "Then, I hope to see you back here soon," he said as he held up his right hand in a high-five gesture and smiled at the satisfied student.

"You just might. Depending upon how things turn out," Terry Grant said prophetically with his well-polished American accent.

He returned the high-five and despite his absolute loathing and contempt of Chip Walker, he managed to grin back at him. He returned to his car and made his way back to his rental cottage.

Chapter 14

The annual 4th of July parade went off without a hitch in the town of Duck. The weather was warm with wall-to- wall sunshine. Mrs. Cullipher and her husband Geoffrey had enjoyed their time as Grand Marshalls. As that week drew to a close it was apparent to all of the restaurant and other business owners that tourist season was nearing its apex. The drive from the Currituck Bridge to town which typically took twenty minutes could take hours if it was a weekend day, as a new batch of cottage renters from all different parts of the U.S. invaded the barrier island in their family vehicles, hoping for sunny skies, with longing anticipation for another carefree and glorious week on the beach basking and playing in the warms waters of the vast Atlantic Ocean.

Back at The Brown Pelican, dinner business was robust as usual this evening. Those who had made reservations at least a week ago were guaranteed to get a table, but walk-ins would not be so fortunate. Last week, Kim Montgomery had called to make a reservation for her and Chip Walker, noting that it was a celebration dinner date and Megan Treadwell gladly booked them a table next to the windows that looked out on the Currituck Sound.

They arrived shortly before eight o'clock in time to watch what would certainly be a colorful sunset amidst cloudless skies. David, one of the restaurant's most loyal and popular servers took their drink order. A Bell's Two-Hearted Ale for Chip, and a vodka tonic for Kim. Outside on the Sound side bar, there was live entertainment. Inside, the couple enjoyed the soft jazz music that head chef Gunny Books personally selected to help create the casual chic atmosphere that he desired for his diners. The place was packed. There were flat screen TV's playing baseball games above the crowded bar. Laughter and the clinking of glasses could be heard, and the aroma of some of the best food served on the Outer Banks wafted through the dining room.

As the drinks were served, they ordered starters of she crab soup for Kim and fried green tomatoes and crab for Chip. David went to turn in the order to the kitchen, and Megan walked over and sat down with them.

"So *this* is the guy that I've been hearing all about," she said as she held out her right hand. Chip shook it.

"Mostly good things I hope?" He said, smiling.

"Nothing but, I should say. It's as if Kim is absolutely giddy when she speaks about you to me. She's never sounded happier," Megan said.

"Look what *I'm* wearing," Kim said as she held out her left hand for Megan to see. She beamed a broad smile.

Megan couldn't help but notice the emerald cut diamond engagement ring on her finger. Megan grabbed her hand gently and pulled it towards her to study the ring.

"Oh my god," Megan said. "It's gorgeous! Congratulations you two! When did this happen?"

"Last night," Chip said.

"It was very romantic, I must admit," Kim said. "Chip took me up to the top of Jockey's Ridge in order to stargaze. At least, that's what he told me about his plans. He got the telescope all set up then he got down on his knee and proposed. He even thought of champagne and two glasses that he stored in his backpack. We're very happy. Thanks, Megan."

"Of course," Megan said. "I'll track down that husband of mine so he can come around and meet Chip and offer his congratulations."

"Great!" Kim said as she pulled out her Android phone. She logged on to the restaurant's Wi-Fi, scanned her messages, and then selected the camera App.

"Would you please take a snapshot of us both?" Kim said.

"Of course," Megan said as she got hold of the device. "Any thoughts on the timing of the wedding?" She asked as she focused the camera.

"October," Kim said. "We want to be leaf peepers in New England during our honeymoon." Megan snapped a picture and returned the phone.

"Autumn in New England is beautiful," Megan said. "Paul and I got a flight to Portland, Maine and drove to Bar Harbor and spent a wonderful long weekend there last fall. I highly recommend it."

"You know that you and I will be talking, girlfriend," Kim said with a smile. "There's so much to plan and arrange. We've got to find a photographer, a caterer, a florist, send out invites, and find a preacher. My head is spinning."

David returned with the starters and set them down on the table.

"Enjoy," he said. "I'll take your dinner orders when you've finished these."

"Thank you, David," Chip said.

"Yes," Megan said. "Enjoy. Your first round of drinks and these starters are on the house with our compliments and congrats."

"Thanks Megan! These look and smell so delicious," Kim said. "Hey. You and Paul wouldn't happen to have any connections over at the Sanderling Resort would you?"

"Maybe. Why? Is that where the wedding's going to be?"

"Yep," Chip said as he took his first fork full of the fried green tomato appetizer. "Right on the beach behind the resort. It's quite a popular spot, so we figure we better get busy booking it soon."

"It's very popular," Megan said. "I could speak with Chef Books about catering your reception? We'd give you a great price. By the way. I remember that I have a short list of contacts at the Sanderling that I keep behind the bar. Kim? Why don't you join me there for a minute?"

"Okay," Kim said. "I'll be back in a minute, dear."

"Take your time," Chip said.

When they reached the bar Megan reached for a small notebook, opened it and showed it to Kim.

"I apologize, but this is just a ruse," Megan said.

"I do have a list of contacts, but moments ago I couldn't help notice that you still have the same phone that David gave to you."

"Yeah," Kim said. "So?"

"Did you at least change your phone number? You don't want David contacting you out of the blue by chance," Megan said.

"O.M.G. You're right," Kim said, revealing some concern on her face.

"I hadn't bothered because I haven't heard from him. And I told you that I love that new phone. But, I'd better do that shouldn't I?"

87

"You and I both know that would be a wise precaution," Megan said. "Change the number at least as soon as you can? Now, let's get back to Chip."

"Thanks for looking out for me," Kim said and smiled.

They returned to the table and found Chip smiling as he chewed on his food.

"If the main dishes here are as good as this appetizer, you've got a deal, Megan," he said. "We'd be honored and obliged to have Chef Books cater our wedding."

"Okay. I'll speak with Mr. Books. Then I'll forward my list of contacts at the Sanderling to Kim and we can see what we come up with," Megan said. "You guys enjoy your food and I'm going to go find Paul."

The seafood entrees were every bit as delicious as the appetizers, and now the couple was enjoying southern pecan pie for dessert.

"The food here is fantastic! What a great meal," Chip said as he raised his glass of wine in a toast.

Kim took up her glass and they toasted the event.

"So," she said. "Since we didn't do much stargazing at all last night, do you want to go out tonight after we get back to your place?"

"I had other plans for the two of us tonight," Chip said.

"Oh?"

"Like working off this dinner in a fun, horizontal sort of way, if you catch my drift?"

"You'll get no arguments from me on that, dear. Tonight feels like such a special night."

"It is special, but, how about tomorrow night instead at around nine? There should be clear skies and a moon out. I could fix us a late dinner snack and we could have a picnic atop Jockey's Ridge under the stars. The park rangers all know me and they'll be cool about that."

"Sounds good. I'll supply the wine," Kim said, raising her glass again.

Kim spotted Megan and Paul maneuvering through the restaurant, checking – in on other guests as they made their way towards their table.

"Oh, good," Kim said. "Megan's found Paul. You'll get to meet him. He's a great guy."

"Chip Walker?" Megan said as they reached the table. She pulled Paul alongside her. "Meet Paul Treadwell, my other half."

"Notice that she didn't say, 'my *better* half,'" Paul said with a smile as he held out his hand.

Chip stood up and chuckled and they shook hands.

"It's a pleasure, Paul. You and Megan have a first class restaurant here," Chip said.

"Most of the credit goes to Gunny Books," Paul said.

"Gunny?"

"He's a Gunnery Sergeant in the U.S. Marines," Paul said. "You noticed that I didn't say that he *was* a Marine, because Gunny would correct me. 'Once a Marine, you're always a Marine,' he says."

"Well he's one hell of a chef," Chip said.

"Yes. We're lucky to have him."

"Please, take a seat," Chip said as he gestured to the two empty chairs. Megan and Paul obliged.

"Megan tells me that you own Nags Head Hang Gliding School?" Paul said.

"Yep. Own it, run it, and teach classes there. It's a passion of mine. Have you and Megan tried it yet?"

Megan and Paul shook their heads.

"I've never had the interest, to be honest. But Paul has been intrigued," Megan said.

"Is that right, Paul?"

Paul nodded.

"Then, what's stopped you?"

Paul jerked his head towards his wife. Megan caught the gesture in a nanosecond.

"Hey there husband," she said. "Don't be putting this on me. Your life insurance is all current, so you go right ahead and break your neck and have fun." She gave him a pleasant push on his shoulder.

"It's perfectly safe," Chip said. "You could take a few tandem flights with me, Paul. Afterwards, you might get hooked. It's a great sport, and with the constant winds on the Outer Banks…" He trailed off and spread his hands.

The four of them spent the next twenty minutes in pleasant conversation as the evening continued. Outside, stars sparkled overhead. The brackish waters of the Currituck Sound gently sluiced against the pilings of the dock and boardwalk, and the daylight creatures of the skies were quiet.

* * * * *

A few miles away, Terry Grant sat back and away from the glowing screen of his laptop. Most of the lights in the place were turned off. Earlier in the day, he had viewed Kim's post on her Facebook page announcing to all her friends that she and Chip were going to enjoy a "celebration dinner" at the Brown Pelican. She even noted the time of the reservation. She went on to post that she would soon clarify what the "celebration" was all about.

Now, after spoofing her Android phone he was able to watch bits and pieces of the celebration dinner sitting in front of his laptop. Naturally, he could hear the entire conversation that she and Chip were having in real time.

"*Bitch*," he said with a hiss as he looked down at the screen.

"How convenient that you kept the phone."

He paused as he let air forcibly out his nostrils like a fire – breathing dragon.

"Right. I think that it's bloody well time that I piss in your trifle, *lovey*," he said out loud as the gears inside his head started spinning like hamsters on wheels.

Chapter 15

The following starlit evening found Chip Walker at Jockey's Ridge with his telescope and backpack. Earlier in the day, Kim had called him to say that she was covering an evening shift for a girl that had called in sick at the Coastal Diamonds and Gems jewelry store. She would meet him after she closed. Chip was setting up his telescope when Hank Atwater, one of the state park's rangers, came by while on patrol.

"Nice night for stargazing, Chip," Hank said.

"That's for sure, Hank. Aren't you guys conducting a stargazing event tonight?" Chip said, referring to the park sponsored summer program.

"Tomorrow night. There will be a lot of parents and kids, so, you're in luck. Tonight you've got the whole area to yourself."

Chip nodded.

"My fiancé will be coming by later. Her name is Kim. I brought along a small picnic for a snack. She loves it up here at night."

"Fiancé, huh? Congrats, Chip!" Hank said as he approached and shook Chip's hand. "When are y'all gonna' tie the knot?"

"Thanks, Hank. October. We haven't set the exact date yet."

"Okay," Hank said. "You'll have to introduce me formally so that I can congratulate her myself. I'll check in with you later, Chip." Hank waved his right arm high in the night sky as he headed down the dune in the direction of the park's headquarters.

Chip had chosen this viewing spot which was about a half mile from the park's visitor center near the landing area used for hang gliding. He was facing due north and behind him about five hundred feet away was the park's ridge top where gliders took off during the day.

Not far away from him, lying prone and hiding under the cover of some scrub forest, an assailant was silently surveying Chip's movements. He was dressed all in black and his head was covered by a black ski mask. In his gloved right hand he held a .22 – caliber Browning Buckmark with an eight inch suppressor, aiming it at Chip as he studied him. His opened hip pack contained a pair of sharp pruning shears. He had watched and listened silently as a park ranger had a short conversation with his mark. He could hear Chip say in the still night air that "Kim" would be coming by "later." So, for the moment the hunter was alone on the sandy hill with his clueless quarry. The night breeze was up and so was his gall as he moved and brought himself up into a crouch position as he decided that it was time for him to make his play.

He stood up and starting pacing towards his victim with his gun arm at his side. His new pair of running shoes gripped the soft, fine sand and gave him a sure step. He studied Chip Walker as he closed range. Walker had made some sort of adjustment to his telescope and then he bent down near his backpack. It looked to the intruder as if he were tying his shoelaces. He was almost on top of him now. He took his left hand and racked the steel slide of the weapon, and pointed it out and downward at Chip Walker.

"Stay very still and don't move a muscle," the assailant said.

Walker was indeed tying his shoe and he looked up at the intruder slowly. He saw the menacing weapon.

"Careful with that thing, mister," Chip said. "Who are you and what do you want?"

He paused with tying his shoe and remained still. His abdomen tightened as he calculated the distance between himself and the intruder. If he sprang up fast enough, he might be able to deflect the gun.

"Who am I, did you say?" The assassin said. "Well I should think that it's rather obvious, but, alright. I'll play along... I'm death, and I'm here to kill you." His British accent was distinctive, Walker thought. He tried to stall the gunman with another question.

"Why would you want to kill me? If it's money you want I can get some for you. Quite a lot, in fact. That's my hang gliding school down there."

Chip jerked his head in the proper direction.

"You can keep the gun on me, I'll let us into my office and you'd be off with a lot of cash money, okay?"

The intruder shook his head.

"No, no, no," he said. "I shan't go on with all the boorish details, *Chip*," he hissed. "But this isn't about money. It's your execution. That's all."

Walker felt increasing fear and dread when he heard the intruder use his own name as well as the word, 'execution.' He had never felt the emotion doom until this moment.

"*Why?*" He said again in genuine astonishment. "What's this all about?"

His voice seemed disconnected from him; his questions sounding hopeless and hanging loose and out of orbit in the night air.

"Because," the intruder said. "Because she said 'no.' And, I don't kill women. Now, keep looking up at me and this will be all over for you in a jiff. Then again, you may close your eyes if you'd prefer. Suit yourself. Night, night, Chip 'ol boy."

Through the opening of his ski mask Chip could see that the assassin was closing his left eye as if he were drawing a careful bead on the end of his gun. He grabbed two handfuls of sand and hurled them up at his intruder's eyes as he sprang up and wheeled to his right in an effort to make his body as narrow a target as possible.

"Fuck!" The intruder yelled as he blindly squeezed the trigger of his weapon.

Chip could feel the shock wave of a bullet tear into the flesh of his outer left shoulder. He was still alive, and his adrenaline was on overload as he turned back and made a grab at his attacker in a mortal effort to disarm him.

"CHIP!!!"

Chip could hear Kim scream as she came into view over the rim of a sand dune.

"Bloody hell!" Chip heard his attacker say as he hit Chip on the side of his head with the butt of his gun. Blood flowed out of the gash in his head and was trickling into his left eye. The attacker turned to run as Walker grabbed him by his hip pack but the intruder was strong, and he pulled away from Walker's grip.

Something flew out of the hip pack. The intruder ran with his gun still in his hand in an easterly direction down towards the road, never once losing his balance.

Walker could feel the throbbing intensity and the burning pain of the gunshot wound. His head throbbed. He cupped his right hand over the wound in his left shoulder and staggered towards Kim. He felt dazed and he was also in a state of total shock and disbelief.

"CHIP!!!" She screamed again.

"Chip?!" Walker could make out Hank Atwater's voice as he joined Kim and ran towards him.

"I'm okay, you two," Chip said. "A crazy fucker *shot* me. I'll be alright. I'll make it."

Atwater yanked out his cell phone and dialed 911.

"I need police and a medic forthwith at Jockey's Ridge state park. A man claims to have been shot, but he appears stable. My name's Atwater. I'm a park ranger. We're about a half mile's walk up from the visitor's center. I'll meet the ambulance when it gets here. Over."

Kim and Hank Atwater reached Chip and they both urged him to sit down on the sand as they waited for help to arrive. Kim was distraught and crying. She held a handkerchief against his head wound and Hank gave him a bandanna to place over the shoulder wound.

"You're a lucky guy and you could probably use some water," Hank said. Chip nodded.

"It's over near the telescope. In my backpack," Chip said. "Thanks, Hank."

"Okay. Stay put. I'll get it." He darted the short distance towards the backpack.

"I'm going to be alright, hon," Chip said to Kim in a strong voice. "I'm sure that I look a lot worse than I really am. But, it was a close call. The crazy fuck said that he had come here to kill me."

"Did you recognize him?" She asked.

He shook his head.

"No. He came out of nowhere. He was dressed all in black and had a black ski mask on. He even said my name," he said as he shook his head and looked down at sand. "My guess is that he must've had a small caliber automatic with a silencer. Still. This hurts like he hit me with a howitzer. *Shit!*"

Hank Atwater returned with a plastic water bottle and gave it to Kim who opened it and poured some into Chip's mouth.

"This may not be the best time to ask," Hank said as a flurry of sirens could be heard fast approaching. "But... Does this item belong to you? I found it near your backpack."

Chip looked over at Hank who was holding a dark metal object in his right hand. Chip studied it. He shrugged and shook his head.

94

"No. It isn't mine. What is it?" Chip said.

"They're pruning shears," Hank said. "I'll turn them over to the police when they get here. I'm going to run down the hill to meet them and the ambulance." He looked over to Kim.

"I'm Hank. Sorry to meet you like this, Kim."

"Me too," she said. "Thank you for helping us."

He nodded and turned away towards the visitor center.

"I'll be right back with the good guys," he said.

Chip looked over at Kim.

"What the *hell* just happened? I mean, how in God's name did this guy know who I am and that I would be out here tonight? And why would he want to kill me? Thank God that you were still at the store."

"The police will find out, and he'll be punished. Right now, I want to get you to the hospital and get you home as soon as we can" she said. "I love you."

"Love you, too," he said, as he squeezed her hand.

Chapter 16

The Outer Banks Hospital is just two miles south of Jockey's Ridge at Mile Post 14. Having undergone surgery for the gunshot wound, Chip was hooked up to an I.V. and resting comfortably in a private recovery room with Kim beside him. The Nags Head police sergeant who was on duty at the hospital contacted his supervisor and they both agreed that Marty Tate needed to be called in on this case. Up until he received the phone call, Tate had been enjoying a peaceful late evening on Roanoke Island with his wife, Elizabeth.

Tate in turn contacted Kenny Smith explaining to him that 'misery loves company.' Kenny would meet him at the hospital. They both knew the victim of the GSW. Chip Walker was a well-known figure to law enforcement in the Outer Banks as he and the police participated or co-sponsored charitable events for the locals throughout the year.

Tate arrived and went inside the hospital lobby. Despite the late hour, there were numerous visitors coming and going. Tate stood alongside a wall near the windows and studied the scene as he waited for Kenny. The lobby's atmosphere exuded a veneer of professionalism, competence and control. However, Tate knew from personal experience that beyond the lobby, in the operating rooms as well as in patient rooms, all phases of the life and death struggle were being experienced in a never- ending circuitous pattern; from babies being born to accidents and illnesses of those once healthy; to sad but expected as well as shocking and non-expected goodbyes. It explained the faces of those that were coming and going tonight. Some were stoic. Others appeared confused and worried. Others looked as if they were making their obligatory evening pilgrimage, their eyes casting thousand yard stares as they walked zombie - like towards the elevators.

Kenny arrived and they in turn were met inside the main lobby by Nags Head police Sgt. Timothy Midgett with whom they had a great working relationship. Midgett was a misnomer considering that he was as big and strong and as quick as an NFL defensive end. His surname was an ancient one on the Outer Banks; some scholars dating it back to the 17th century. It was as common a name here as "Smith" was on the mainland.

"Sorry to call you out so late, gentlemen," Midgett said. "But, considering the victim of tonight's shooting is Chip Walker, we thought you'd like to talk with him."

"This sucks," Kenny said. "Chip's a great guy."

"Thanks for calling us, Tim," Tate said. "How's he doing?"

"He's fine. You know Chip. He's tough. He's more disturbed by the circumstances. He'll tell you." Midgett said.

"Let's go over here and talk before you go see him yourselves."

He nodded his head towards a sectional sofa near the windows. They all took a seat. Midgett placed the patrol briefcase that he was carrying down in front of him. He opened it and then handed over two clear plastic bags, one with a bullet inside. One bag was given to him by the O.R.' physician at Chip's nurse's station. The other bag was given to him by the police crime scene techs. Tate took them.

"It's a small caliber bullet that they removed from Chip's outer shoulder. Most likely a .22," Midgett said, pointing to the bag. "In the other bag is a shell casing found at the scene. It's probably from the same gun."

"Sure looks that way to me," Tate said as he handed them over to Kenny Smith.

"Evidence is all signed and sealed by the medical staff," Midgett said.

"Chip's damned lucky that he walked away with a flesh wound. His masked attacker more or less had him dead to rights. Anyway, I wanted you both to see the other item that was found by the park ranger near Chip's things on Jockey's Ridge. Take a look."

He reached inside his patrol briefcase and removed the pair of pruning shears that were found by Hank Atwater on the sandy ridge. The item was also bagged.

"Well *fuck*-a-doodle-do," Tate said as he briefly studied the tool inside the bag before he handed it over to Kenny.

"Son of a bitch," Kenny said.

"Anything remarkable about that tool that you'd care to share, guys?" Midgett said.

Tate looked over at Smith. Kenny nodded, then looked back over at Timothy Midgett.

"We're investigating an open unsolved homicide that happened last month on Roanoke," Smith said.

"The psychologist that was found shot on his yacht?" Midgett asked.

"Yeah," Tate said. "Shot inside his boat. Go on, Kenny."

"Right. Well, the victim's wedding ring finger was removed post mortem by what the M.E. thinks could be…"

"A pair of pruning shears," Midgett said, finishing Smith's sentence. "And tonight there was the attempted murder of Chip. Chip told me that he grabbed the guy and that this item flew out of the hip sack that his attacker was wearing. Son of a bitch…"

"Yep," Tate said. "This could be our guy. Same caliber bullet, and now this unusual paraphernalia found at tonight's crime scene. Depending on what Chip tells us, I'd say that the odds are pretty good that this is the guy we've been after."

"There's something else you two may not know yet," Midgett said.

"Do tell," Kenny Smith said.

"Chip recently got engaged."

Tate pursed his lips and looked over to Smith who was rubbing his chin with his right hand.

"You don't say," Smith said. "Who's the lucky girl?"

"She's a stunner," Midgett said. "Her name is Kim Montgomery. She's upstairs with Chip now."

"I've met this woman," Tate said to Midgett. He looked over at Kenny. "I met her at the Brown Pelican. She's a good friend of Megan Treadwell. And yes. She's pretty."

"Okay," Smith said.

"Ms. Montgomery arrived on the scene as Chip was struggling with his attacker. But again, I'll let them tell you their story. Just out of curiosity though, was the psychologist who was shot also engaged or married?" Midgett said.

"He was engaged to be married," Smith said.

"A coincidence?" Midgett said.

"Not a fucking chance, is what I think," Tate said. "And, who the hell takes a pair of pruning shears to a shooting?"

"There's that," Midgett said. "The pruners look clean."

"We'll dust 'em and get the lab to look for trace elements of blood. If there is and the trace matches up with the late good doctor…" Kenny said as he spread his hands.

"Then you've confirmed that it's the same guy," Midgett said.

Smith nodded.

"And confirmed that this sick bastard is still in the wind," Tate said. "Thanks Tim. This has been extremely helpful-to perhaps both cases."

"You're welcome, Marty. Chip remembers quite a bit about what his masked attacker said before he took his shot. I think that you'll find it compelling. You should also know that both Chip and Kim are pretty convinced that the attacker was someone that she dated for a few weeks over a month ago."

"Oh?" Tate said. "Why do they think that?"

"They'll tell you the exact words that the attacker used to the best of Chip's memory, but, it was the attacker's accent that he found distinctive. The attacker had a British accent."

"Really?" Kenny Smith said.

"Yep," Midgett said. "Chip said the guy sounded like he just jumped off a double decker bus at Piccadilly Circus. Not a cockney accent, either. The guy sounded to Chip like he was upper - crust British. Not too many of them down here in the Banks. The guy that Kim dated also had a British accent."

Marty glanced over his shoulder at Kenny Smith who was rubbing his chin again.

"Let's head upstairs," he said to Smith.

Smith and Tate shook hands with Midgett and they headed for the elevator.

99

Chapter 17

Tate and Smith found Chip and Kim watching The Weather Channel as they entered the room. They both turned to look at the visitors as Kim muted the sound of the TV on the remote.

"Marty! Kenny!" Chip said as he held out his right hand into the air. Kim smiled.

"Good to see you in one piece, Chip," Tate said as he gave him a fist bump. "Hello again, Ms. Montgomery. Congratulations. I heard that the two of you are now engaged?"

"Hello Sheriff Tate, and please call me Kim. Yes. We're lucky to still be looking forward to that wonderful day. I'm Kim," she said as she held out her hand towards Kenny Smith.

"Nice to meet you, Kim," Kenny said as he shook her hand and introduced himself. He looked over at Chip and like Tate, gave him a fist bump.

"I hope that it's not too late in the evening for you to speak to us about what happened at Jockey's Ridge?" Tate said.

"Sgt. Midgett said that it would be important for me to tell you the whole story, so, no, it's not too late. Where would you like me to begin?" Chip said. "Why don't you both take a seat?"

Tate and Smith did as invited when Marty asked the first question.

"What brought you out to Jockey's Ridge tonight?"

"I really enjoy stargazing from up there and so that's what I had set out to do tonight. I had my telescope set up and I had shared a few words with Hank Atwater, one of the park rangers, right before this guy showed up."

"Who, besides Kim, knew that you were going up there tonight?" Kenny asked.

"Not a soul. That's one of the creepiest parts about this whole episode, guys. No one knew except for Kim and Hank."

"Okay," Marty said. "Walk us through exactly what happened as you remember it? Take it slow. We're going to be taking some notes."

"Well, it's like I just said. I had just set up my telescope and I had some brief words with Hank about the park's stargazing program and this guy appears dressed all in black like some kind of ninja assassin."

"Which direction did he come from?" Tate asked.

"I don't know," Chip said. "I was bent down tying my shoes when he came up to me. By the time I looked up he was there in front of me."

"Did he have his weapon drawn?" Smith asked.

Chip nodded.

"The doctor told me that it was a small caliber bullet that they removed from my shoulder, but, when I was kneeling down and looking up at that thing, it seemed as big as a bazooka. Scared the shit out of me."

"What happened next?" Tate asked.

"I remember asking him who the hell he was," Chip said.

"Did he answer?" Tate said.

"Yeah. He said that he was death and that he was there to kill me."

Kim put her right hand over her mouth and shook her head.

"Death? Is that what he called himself?" Smith asked.

"Yes. I was stalling for time and offered him money. He said that he wasn't interested in money and that tonight it was time for my execution." Chip said. "He also called me by my first name."

Tate and Smith nodded.

"Was there anything else you remember him saying?" Smith asked.

"Yes," Chip said. "When I asked him why he was doing this he said it was because she said no and that he didn't kill women."

"Say that again?" Tate said.

"It's what he said. "He said I'm going to kill you because she said no, and he didn't kill women."

"Did you have any idea what he was talking about?" Tate said.

"None," Chip said. "I was scared and I was trying to figure out a way to not get shot, but I know that's what he said. Then he told me that I could look up at him or close my eyes. That's when I knew he was getting ready to pull the trigger and I made my play. I grabbed some sand in each of my hands and threw it towards his eyes as I stood up and made a lunge for the gun. I remember pivoting to my right to give him a slim profile to shoot at.

101

I guess it worked. He screamed, 'fuck!' We struggled a little. He hit me with the butt of his gun. He said, 'bloody hell,' and started to run. I grabbed him by the hip pack that he was carrying and something flew out and he ran down the hill. That's when Kim and Hank showed up."

"I know that he was all in black, but, could you make out what he looked like in terms of height or shape? Anything distinctive about his voice?" Tate asked.

Chip rubbed the bandage on his head and started to nod and he looked over at Kim.

"He had a British accent, that's for sure. The way that he said, 'bloody hell' was very distinctive. He was about Kenny's height. Slim, but agile and quick. Probably younger than you or me."

"I think that I know who did this to Chip," Kim said looking straight into Tate's eyes.

"Who then?" Tate said.

"A guy that I dated earlier this summer. I met him on a dating website. He was in his late 20's. He had a British accent. He proposed marriage to me and I said, 'no.'"

"Okay," Tate said. "Name?"

"He called himself David Wiggins. Very mysterious guy. I never felt completely at ease in his presence."

Marty and Kenny heard the name of the character that Anne Scarborough had so thoroughly described to them a month ago. They didn't register recognition.

Kim continued.

"Like I said, he was a strange guy. He spent cash everywhere we went. No credit or debit cards. He drove an expensive looking car and he even paid cash when we went to a gas station. He was never clear about what he did for a living. I never even got to know where he lived. I was never at his *flat*, as he called it."

"Do you have any pictures of this guy?" Tate asked.

"No," Kim said. "He had the same build that Chip's attacker had. The age is about right and the accent. But, it's what he said to Chip that sticks in my craw. He told Chip that he was going to kill him tonight because 'she said no.' I think that he was telling Chip about me turning down his offer of marriage. That's too big of a coincidence if you ask me."

"How did he take your rejection?" Smith asked.

"Like a perfect gentlemen," Kim said. "He had even bought and engagement ring and proposed over a dinner date. I was shocked. When I told him my answer, he put the ring away and said something like, 'no hard feelings,' and 'best of luck,' and all that. I've never heard from him since and that was well over a month ago."

"Are you positive that he called himself David Wiggins?" Tate said.

"The website where I found him simply listed his picture and first name. I gave him my last name on our second date. In hindsight, that was probably very stupid of me because he could go look me up on Facebook and Twitter and Instagram and so on. I had a feeling that he did. Anyway, when I asked about his last name, that's what he gave me. I tried looking him up on Facebook and other social media sites, but, I couldn't find a trace of him. So, I'm assuming that he gave me a *false* last name. Hell... David may not even be his real *first* name. The guy was very secretive."

"That could explain a few things," Tate said as he looked directly at Kenny.

"Yes," Kenny said.

"Could this be the guy who attacked me?" Chip said as he held Kim's hand in his.

"It's possible given what he said about his motive for killing you," Tate said.

"Kim," Kenny said. "Can you recall anything else about this Wiggins guy? You mentioned a car that he drove. Do you remember what kind?"

"It was a newer model white BMW," she said without hesitation.

Kenny looked back over at Marty and nodded before he made another note on his pad of paper.

Do you remember the name of the dating website where you came across this David Wiggins?" Tate asked.

"Are you ready for this?" Kim said. "It's called, 'Happily-Ever-After.com.' I'm no longer a member, obviously." She smiled over at Chip.

Both Tate and Smith remained poker faced upon hearing the name of the website that Anne Scarborough had also previously identified.

"I get the feeling by your questions that you guys are trying real hard not to tell us something," Chip said.

"We're the cops, Chip," Tate said. "That means we can't tell you everything especially when we don't know everything ourselves. Still… I can tell you that we've come across this man's name, description and the name of that website in the course of investigating a different case."

"No shit," Chip said.

"Have you found him and questioned him?" Kim said.

"No," Tate said. "When you gave us this name tonight and told us that you couldn't track him down, that's when I said 'this could explain a few things' to Kenny a few moments ago. We believe the same thing that you do. This guy is using an alias. We've not been able to locate him."

"Did you investigate the website?" Chip asked.

"Good thinking, Chip," Tate said. "We did. We also petitioned a judge for a subpoena to look into this guy's internet domain, or whatever you call it. The judge turned us down saying that we didn't have enough evidence to obtain the warrant."

"Is that true?" Kim said.

"Yes. What we had – up until tonight – was circumstantial and based upon a second party's hunch. Tonight changes things I think, Kenny," Tate said.

"Agreed," Smith said.

"Okay," Tate said as he stood up. Smith followed his lead.

"We have a sketch that was drawn by our police artist that I'd like you to see first thing in the morning, Kim?" Tate said. "It's based on a description that a woman gave us last month. She too described this guy as mysterious."

"Did this guy propose marriage to her, too?" Kim said.

"Like I told Chip," Tate said. "We're the cops. We can't tell you everything."

He smiled at her and she smiled back.

"Fair enough," she said.

"We've got enough to start running some things down, thanks to you two. Nice job of thinking fast and defending yourself, Chip. This guy put you in a highly dangerous situation and you found a way to get out of it and stay alive. Then again, I could have

104

told this asshole that you'd be the wrong guy to fuck with." Tate winked at Chip. "No offense, Kim."

"None taken," she said. "Thanks for getting here so soon tonight, sheriff."

"Yeah. Thanks, Marty," Chip said.

Tate gave Kim his official card with the Manteo address. He gave another one to Chip.

"Give me a call if anything else comes to mind?" Tate said.

"Will do," Chip said.

"We'll find ourselves out. Have a quiet evening, you two," Tate said. "We'll see you tomorrow morning, Kim? Ask for Peggie when you get to headquarters."

Back downstairs in the lobby, Tate and Smith took a seat on a sofa in order to debrief their interview while the facts were fresh in their minds.

Tate looked out across the lobby and put his elbows on his knees and locked his large hands together as he leaned forward.

"David - fucking - Wiggins, my ass," he said looking straight ahead.

"He's a clever bastard, I'll give him that. Whatever his real name is," Kenny said.

Tate nodded still looking ahead.

"Well luckily, Mr. Criminal Genius fucked up tonight. We've got a bullet, a witness, a possible former girlfriend, some pruning shears, a description of his overall build and a description of his voice and accent. We've got a white BMW being mentioned again. And, a possible peek into his motives for going after these two men. If Kim and Chip are right, and *if* it's the same guy. And my gut tells me that he is," Tate said.

"Let's get those shears over to the lab A.S.A.P., Kenny. And let's petition that judge about the website again."

"Roger that," Kenny said.

"If we get lucky, we'll find some trace elements on those shears, and if we get *real* lucky, we might be able to obtain some digital breadcrumbs via that website that will lead us to this guy."

"Agreed. It still bothers me as to how he knew where Chip would be tonight," Kenny said.

Tate looked back over at him.

"I think that Ms. Kim herself may have posted something on Facebook that this guy latched on to. A lot of smart people post totally too much information about themselves and what they're up to on social media, not thinking that there might be predators out there looking for a way to take advantage of them. She admitted that she gave him her genuine last name early on. I agree with her assessment that that was mistake."

"I hadn't considered that," Kenny said.

"It's late," Tate said as he surveyed the lobby. "I'm going home and I'm going to try to get some sleep. We've got an early day tomorrow."

"Okay," Kenny said. "I'll stop at Dunkin' Donuts on the way in tomorrow and fetch us some extra-large coffees."

"Don't forget the sinkers." Tate said with a smile.

"Got it. Plain for me and strawberry- filled for you?"

"Good man," Tate said.

Chapter 18

Before sunup the next day, Richard Dolenz had packed a third suitcase into the trunk of his car. He went back inside the beach cottage to look around one last time. He made his way to the kitchen and looked to his right towards the living room. Through the grand wall of windows that faced the ocean he could make out the rising sun. He also saw the outline of a man sitting quietly in a high-back chair looking out to sea. From the familiar outline of his head Richard knew that it was Terry Grant, and he relaxed and refocused as he made his way to the island counter.

"I didn't expect to see you here so early in the morning," Richard said.

"Oh, I've been up half the night, so what's another hour or two?" Terry said. "Where do you think you're going, by the way?"

"I'm going back to Richmond. That should be obvious by now. The wedding photography business isn't making me dick, nor are the freelance gigs. With dear old mum's allowance dwindling, I can't afford this place as well as the flat in Richmond. So, I'm off, old chap."

Terry hadn't moved a muscle. He just sat in the pre-dawn light looking out the window.

"Are you sure that you couldn't rustle up a few quid and stay on for a little longer?" Terry said.

"No. Now's the time to be leaving this place. Besides, in a few weeks' time the hurricanes will be blowing in the Atlantic, and I'd much rather be on dry land, thank you very much."

"I don't believe you," Terry said.

"What don't you believe?"

"That the lack of money is the only thing that's making you leave. I for one, fancy this place. I've been having so much fun with the mayhem and mischief that I've discovered here."

"At least one of us is happy. But, I'm the one who has to pay the rent and the bills," Richard said as he opened and closed a few cupboards. He found a half bag of Doritos and put them on the counter to take with him. He opened and closed the refrigerator. It was still as empty as it was when he awoke this morning.

"I'd like to talk about last night," Terry said.

Richard paused. He looked across the room and saw that Terry hadn't moved.

"There's nothing to talk about. Now it's getting on in the day and I need to get a move on. There's less cops and traffic about this early in the morning."

"That's important to you, isn't it?" Terry said.

"Yes," Richard said. "Now, are you coming along?"

"I'll be along. Presently," Terry said as he continued looking out the window.

Richard shook his head, and after making another last pass around the entire place, he started heading for the main door. When he glanced back at the living room, it was empty.

Chapter 19

Several days later, heavy rains were falling all up and down the Outer Banks as a low pressure system was moving in from the southwest, making its way out to the open sea. During tourist season especially, steady rains along the beach were an added boon to the local restaurants, historical sights, art and jewelry galleries, and the small shops that sold various OBX tchotchkes. Today was such a day. The shops and restaurants were as saturated with human traffic as the sidewalks and the streets were with running water, as cars with out-of-state license plates jockeyed for precious parking spots in towns like Corolla and Duck, and Kitty Hawk and Nags Head.

Back in Manteo on Roanoke Island, Sheriff Marty Tate was looking out his office window as the cleansing rain sheeted down against the panes of glass. Tate liked the rain for a variety of reasons, not the least of which that it had a neutralizing effect against some of the more common crimes. This summer in particular, and for no special reason, a rash of break-ins were occurring on sunny days in Nags Head and Kitty Hawk. Most of the crimes were items of value being stolen out of tourist's unlocked cars and rental homes. Despite signs plastered in every open, public space warning residents and tourists alike about the risk of leaving their car and/or their houses unlocked, people were nevertheless neglectful to take heed, and as a consequence they and some of their prized possessions were parted from one another. Luckily, along with the assistance of some paid informants, the Dare County Sheriff's office was able to locate several of the more expensive items that had been looted and had returned them to their rightful owners. The offending thieves were arrested, charged, booked and placed inside holding cells of what had fondly become known to the locals as "Marty Tate's Hilton," otherwise known as the Dare County Detention Center.

As she had promised days earlier, Kim Montgomery had stopped into Tate's office and was shown the sketch of a certain 'David Wiggins' that the police artist had made based upon the description that was given by Anne Scarborough weeks prior. Tate was now recalling her visit as he looked out at the falling rain.

She confirmed that the image was as close to a recollection that she had of the same man and could offer no changes to the sketch. She asked a few questions about the man and about Tate's other investigation that had brought forth the sketch. Tate was customarily compelled to decline to answer her questions in light of the two cases that he now viewed as a double helix. The murder of Dr. Phillip McCleney and the attempted murder of Chip Walker. And, if he added the case of Kevin Berkley in Virginia, a triple helix.

She had remarked to Tate before leaving his office that in some way the sketch appeared more life-like than a photo to her because the artist had really captured the man's eyes. In real life, she had found them to be both spellbinding as well as chilling. She had sounded a bit philosophical to Tate that morning as she went on to say that 'David' was himself a bit like the Roman god, Janus, who is depicted with two faces. Seen through the centuries as the god of beginnings and endings, Janus was as well the god of duality, and doorways and passages.

She recalled his outward charm, but sensed that he had a dark side. She also hoped that Tate would bring an end to the man's criminal behaviors as both she and Chip were convinced wholeheartedly that this was the man responsible for the attack on Jockey's Ridge.

Tate couldn't guarantee an apprehension, but he did guarantee his resolve to follow the evidence where it led him. Against his judgement, he also reminded her that since the attacker had tried to kill Chip, one of his friends, that the case was personal. She understood his meaning immediately; Tate had developed a real hard-on for capturing 'David Wiggins.' He wouldn't let it go.

She was optimistic when she left that morning and she told Tate that she and Chip were in the market for a good wedding photographer if he knew of anyone with such talents. He remembered grinning back at her and telling her that the only one he could recall was the one that took the photos at his wedding 'back in the late Mesozoic era.' She had laughed at his humor and had promised to stay in touch if something else occurred to Chip about the night of the attack. A loud knock at his office door brought Tate back to present reality.

Tate turned in his swivel chair to see that it was Kenny Smith standing in the doorway with two manila folders in his right hand.

"Well, it looks like you still have a lot of juice when it comes to the crime lab," he said. "The results from the analysis of the hand pruners are in this report."

He waved one of the folders above his head.

"Enough with the foreplay, Kenny," Tate said. "What's it say?"

Kenny Smith entered the office and took a seat opposite Tate and placed the folder on top of the desk in front of his boss. Tate perused the contents as Smith summarized the findings.

"Even though the pruners were evidently wiped clean, the lab found trace elements of blood and DNA."

"And?" Tate said as he looked up at Smith.

"It's a match with Dr. McCleney's. The guy who killed the good doctor aboard his yacht was the same guy that tried to kill Chip Walker on Jockey's Ridge. It's got to be him."

"Aboard the doctor's *boat*," Tate said with a grin on his face.

"Whatever," Smith said. "I'm afraid we weren't as lucky with coming up with anything substantial from the "Happily- Ever-After" website search."

"After all that trouble we went to in order to get the expedited search warrant? Shit," Tate said.

"I know," Smith said. "Everything that Norm found out while conducting the search is in this other report."

Smith put the other folder down on the desk in front of Tate. Norm Henderson was the trusted Dare County Cyber forensics officer that Smith was referring to.

"Norm has concluded that both Anne Scarborough and Kim Montgomery were the on-line victims of catfishing," Smith said.

"Tell me that again - in plain English, please?" Tate said.

"Sorry," Smith said. "Catfishing is a type of deceptive activity where a person creates a fake identity on a social networking site for nefarious purposes."

"Uh-huh. Well, we already suspected that," Tate said. "What exactly did Norm find out?"

"This guy set up his account under the name of David Wiggins using a stolen credit card number."

"Of course he did, the scrupulous fuck," Tate said.

"Oh, he's more scrupulous than you think. There's more."

"Do tell."

"On his account profile he listed his general interests and hobbies such as photography. Nothing out of the ordinary. So, Norm gets curious. He was able to trace the I.P. address of the computer that he used to set up the account to a cyber café in Richmond, Virginia."

"He didn't even use his own computer or his own credit card?"

"Nope. And when he deleted the account, which was 72 hours before his attempted murder of Chip Walker, he deleted the photograph of himself from the website."

"How the hell could he do that?"

"Norm is pretty confident that this guy is no slouch when it comes to cyber intelligence."

"He's a hacker?"

"Yeah," Smith said. "And a damned good one, according to Norm. He got back into the website and shot his picture off into cyberspace Neverland, and then he inserted a message for us to find instead."

"I'm not following you."

"He inserted a text message at the bottom of his deleted profile. Only a guy like Norm Henderson would be able to find this, and this guy apparently knew that."

Tate made an impatient *let's get on with it* rolling gesture with his right hand.

"The message read, 'To all my friends at the Cop Shop. Good luck trying to find me.'"

"I probably already know the answer to my next question, but I'll ask it anyway… Was Norm able to locate the I.P. address of the computer this guy used to do all this?"

"No. This guy knows how to cover his digital tracks on the internet. It's as if this guy didn't seem to care if a guy like Norm traced the original computer activity to a cyber café in Richmond, but he covered his comings and goings on the website very carefully after he set up his profile."

"How were women like Anne and Kim supposed to contact this guy based on his dating website profile?"

"Initially, they would connect with him through his own personal website, and then by phone. Probably burner phones that he's already thrown away."

112

"Let me guess," Tate said. "His website doesn't exist anymore either?"

"Nope. Gone with the wind."

"Shit," Tate said again as he closed the folder and sat back in his chair.

"Sorry," Smith said. "Like I said at the start we got nothing substantial out of the website search."

"Not exactly, 'nothing,'" Tate said.

"What do you mean?"

"The cyber café is located in Richmond, right?"

"Right." Smith said.

"Anne Scarborough said that this guy had a Virginia driver's license and that his car had Virginia plates. It's time that we get everything that we've learned over to Jared McClure." Tate said.

"Agreed."

"It appears that the guy we're after proposed marriage to two different women that he wasn't intimate with, then he took the rejection of his marriage proposal just like a complete gentleman. But then takes a run at their new fiancés. In this first case, he kills the guy. In the second case, he was trying to kill Chip. Paul Treadwell suggested that this could be this guy's motive."

"I remember that you mentioned that," Kenny said.

"I think that we need to know more about this mystery guy that we're chasing," Tate said as he opened up his desk drawer and took out an old-fashioned Rolodex. He thumbed through it and took out a business card and handed it over to Smith.

"Remember this guy?" Tate said.

Kenny Smith looked down at the card. It read: "Special Agent William Etheridge; Behavioral Analysis Unit; Federal Bureau of Investigation; Quantico, Virginia."

"Bill? Of course I remember him. His hometown is Wanchese."

Wanchese is the site of the first fishing village on the southern end of Roanoke Island. It was named after Wanchese, the last known ruler of the Roanoke Native American tribe encountered by English colonists in the sixteenth century.

"He was our FBI instructor at the National Academy Program in Quantico. He's the profiler," Smith said.

"Exactly," Tate said. "When he gave me his card he said that if we ever got jammed up, that I should give him a call."

"I'd say that we're jammed up here," Smith said. Tate nodded.

"Let me call him and give him an overview of what we've got going with the two cases here as well as the case that McClure is working on. If he wants more, I'll provide it."

"You're hoping that he can put together a profile on this guy? You think that might help us?"

"Shit, I don't know, Kenny." Tate said as he stood up and walked over to the window. The rain had stopped outside.

"I'd like to hear whatever Bill could tell us about the kind of monster that we're chasing here," Tate said as he continued to gaze out his window. "Besides, he's a straight shooter and a fellow Outer Banker. You remember he's stopped by here a couple of times on his way down to Wanchese?"

"I do," Kenny Smith said. "He owns a fishing boat there. I think calling him is worth a shot."

"I should tell McClure that we're seeking out Bill's expertise," Tate said as he returned to his desk and sat down across from Kenny.

"He might get a little nervous that we're reaching out to the Feds."

"Only if I put it to him that way. I'll give Jared our connection and background with Bill during our training at the academy, and that he's our neighbor of sorts. He should be fine with it. Hell, I'll invite him in on any discussions we have." Tate said as he took back the business card from Smith.

"Did the lab find any other blood traces on the pruners?" Tate asked.

"Yes, they did. You're thinking that the other trace elements could match Kevin Berkley's blood type and DNA from a year ago in Virginia?"

"Make the call to Jared and get the blood type of the victim. If it's another trace match, it will be another nail in the coffin for this killer when we catch him. And that would be a darlin' thing," Tate said.

"Will do," Kenny Smith said as he stood and left the office.

114

Tate went back to the file related to the dating website and found the 'David Wiggins' message that Norm had underlined in his report:

To all my friends at the Cop Shop. Good luck trying to find me.

"Fuck you," Tate said out loud in the empty office. "And I'm certainly *not* your god-damned friend, you total piece of shit."

Tate closed the file and reached for his phone.

Chapter 20

One week later in the first part of August, Lt. Jared McClure and Trooper Fred Drury were seated in a small conference room inside the Virginia State Police Area 14 office in Luray, Virginia, together with Marty Tate and Kenny Smith. In the middle of the table sat a Polycom SoundStation EX conference phone. Two days earlier, the Dare County Medical Examiner concluded that the other blood trace found on the pruning shears that were left behind by the attacker on Jockey's Ridge matched with Kevin Berkley's blood type as supplied by the Virginia State Police Crime Lab. The unknown subject that the four officers were pursuing was a fugitive known to them as David Wiggins, and in the space of just a little over a year, he had killed two men and had attempted to kill a third.

Now, they waited for the call that was to come at the top of the hour from William Etheridge, based in Quantico, Virginia.

"We're circling back soon to interview Ms. Mary Brennen," McClure said.

"Remind me again of who she is?" Tate said.

"She was the victim's - Kevin Berkley's - fiancé at the time of his death last year," McClure said. "Given what you guys learned about the unknown subject from Kim Montgomery and Chip Walker, it makes sense. We had contacted her after we positively identified Kevin Berkley's remains, but now we have new questions about men that she may have been serious with before she got engaged to Berkley while they were attending UVA. I'm looking forward to what Special Agent Etheridge has to tell us."

Tate and Smith nodded.

"He doesn't have a whole lot to work with and this is a rush job," Tate said.

"I know," McClure said. "But if he's as impressive as you and Kenny say, we're willing to invest the time in this conference call."

Trooper Drury nodded in agreement. The phone rang and McClure reached over and pushed a button.

"State Trooper Jared McClure speaking," McClure said in a steady voice.

"William Etheridge here," the voice replied over the phone.

"I've got Marty Tate and Kenny Smith and Trooper Fred Drury here. Thanks for making time for us, Special Agent Etheridge."

"Call me Bill? Believe me, I've been called a whole lot worse," Etheridge said.

"O.K.," McClure said smiling.

"Hey Bill," Tate said, and he was followed by a greeting from Kenny Smith.

"Hey guys," Etheridge replied back. "I'm coming down to Wanchese in a few weeks while the blues are still running if you'd like to tag along?"

Etheridge was referring to the fish that have bluish green upper backs that fade to gray/silver down their sides to a white belly. As they grow older they live in small packs and feed on schools of forage fish and occasionally attack ruthlessly in a frenzy called a "blitz." The Outer Banks are famous for blitzes when packs of bluefish chase many species of fish through the surf zone onto the beach.

"Sounds good," Tate said. "Keep us posted? I really appreciate you taking time out of your day for us, Bill. Have you been able to come up with some thoughts about our unknown subject?"

"I will and I have," Etheridge said.

"You were able to come up with a profile so quickly?" Trooper Drury asked after he introduced himself.

"Sort of, Fred," Etheridge said. "I'd call it 'profile lite.' Based on the evidence found at the crime scenes that you guys have provided as well as your interview with witnesses Montgomery and Walker, I have arrived at a basic offender description. I prefer to think about the work that I do here at the Bureau as criminal investigative analysis, but, you can call it 'profiling' if you'd like."

"Got it," Drury said.

"So, how would you describe our offender?" McClure asked.

"I think that he's a genuine fucked-up, walking, talking creepazoid," Etheridge shot back without hesitation.

McClure hit the mute button on the phone and looked over at Tate with a large grin on his face.

"Hey," he said to Tate. "I like this guy already, Marty."

117

"I thought that you would," Tate said. McClure hit the mute button again.

"So this guy of ours is nuts?" McClure asked.

"No," Etheridge said. "Which makes him more dangerous and hard as hell to catch. I'll tell you up front that my observations are probably not going to help you catch this guy. But, if he's apprehended, this background information might help you to get him to open up during an interrogation."

"Okay," Tate said. "Fair enough."

"Jared," Etheridge continued. "The reason why I say that this guy is not insane is based on his highly organized crimes. Organized crimes are premeditated and carefully and shrewdly planned. Therefore, little evidence is found at the crime scene. At the marina where Dr. McCleney was executed Marty and Kenny found a bullet cartridge casing, for instance. Not a lot to go on. The guy you're after knows right from wrong and shows no remorse to his victims. The comments that he made to Chip Walker are a classic example of that characteristic. On the other hand, disorganized criminals may be mentally ill or on drugs or alcohol and they typically leave behind fingerprints and/or blood. They don't plan their crimes."

"I see," McClure said. Etheridge continued.

"Serial killers such as this guy that we're talking about typically present a public face that appears to be good or even charming and at the same time he is nurturing a dark side that allows murderous fantasies free reign. Think Ted Bundy."

"A Janus figure," Tate said.

"Exactly, Marty. Two faces. Two sides to them. They typically have painful memories that come from abuse or disappointment or humiliation, and they turn to murderous fantasies to comfort themselves. They might even develop an alternative identity that makes them feel more powerful or having more status."

"We know that his real name isn't David Wiggins," Kenny Smith said.

"Exactly," Etheridge said. "That could be this guy's alternate identity."

"I sent you my report via e-mail prior to our call. Did it come through alright, Jared?" Etheridge asked.

"It did and I made copies for all of us. Would you prefer that we review this now?" McClure said.

118

"You most certainly may while I summarize," Etheridge said, as the four men around the conference table flipped through the report.

"First off, I'd say that this David Wiggins is highly intelligent. His computer hacking skills are first rate. In addition to his false identity, he uses only cash or in one case, a stolen credit card. Again, that's smart if he doesn't wish to leave a paper trail. He told one of the women that he was a venture capitalist. Anne Scarborough and Kim Montgomery both said that he appeared to be a big spender with a fancy European car and presented them with a fancy engagement ring. He proposed marriage to both these women even though he hadn't been intimate with either. Have I got it right so far?"

"Yes," The four men replied back in unison.

"Marty… Did either woman report that he said, 'I love you' with any frequency?" Etheridge asked.

Tate turned to Kenny who paged through the interview notes made with both women before he answered.

"No," Kenny said. "They said that he told them that they would make the perfect wife."

"Thanks Kenny," Etheridge said. "That bolsters my hypothesis that we'll get to in a minute. That this David Wiggins may have perceived intimacy before marriage to these women as violating his vision of viewing them as perfect or virginal."

"That's either way old-fashioned or creepy as hell," Tate said.

"I recommend that we stick with 'creepy' when it comes to this character," Etheridge said. "So, they turn his preposterous proposal down, and instead of getting furious, he seems polite, but continues to stalk these women literally or most likely through the use of cell phones or the internet."

"Wait a minute," Tate said as looked over at Kenny. "Didn't Anne Scarborough tell us that David Wiggins had gifted her a cell phone?"

"Sure enough," Smith said.

"There you go," Etheridge said. "Android phones can be hacked."

"We'd better circle back to see if he gave Kim Montgomery a phone," Tate said. "If so, we need to warn both women about this."

119

"Will do," Kenny said as he made a note.

"Sorry about the interruption, Bill." Tate said. "Please continue."

"As I was saying, he then finds their next serious love interest, and executes them and mutilates their bodies by removing their wedding ring fingers post mortem."

"That's our sick unknown subject alright," McClure said.

"Actually, I think that he's hoping that this detail gets back to his former girlfriend or better yet, that she finds the body and sees the mutilation with her own eyes," Etheridge explained. "It serves the purpose of making his symbolic *Fuck You* gesture even more ironic and terrifying."

"It's ironic alright," Tate said. "What did you make from the police artist drawing that I sent you?"

"I looked at it last after I estimated that this man to be in his late twenties. The sketch shows a man in his prime. I'd say that he's educated, and that he feels that women owe him whatever he wants. He was more than likely spoiled and grew up as a single child inside an affluent family. He was, in my estimation, conversely withheld from getting everything that he wanted from a strong, authority figure."

"You're *not* going to say that it was his *mother*," Tate said with a sarcastic tone.

"I won't have to. Now that *you've* said it Marty," Etheridge shot back.

The other three officers at the table laughed while Tate pursed his lips and shook his head in a good natured fashion.

"It's always the mother," Tate said as he held his hands up in the air. "It's always the mother when it comes to these frickin' freaks."

The others in the room nodded in agreement.

After spending a little more time walking the four police officers through the more technical aspects of his report, Etheridge was ready to summarize and provide his working hypothesis about the unknown subject's motives and possible future behavior.

"In conclusion, it's my opinion that this David Wiggins is not interested in marriage," Etheridge said in a calm fashion.

"What?!" The four officers in the room said simultaneously.

"He doesn't want to marry them. He wants to hurt them. The marriage proposal is a charade and part of his fantasy scheme. He knows full well that these women will say 'no' to his proposal of marriage. He hasn't been intimate with any of them. The engagement ring that he shows them is like a form of bait. He's holding it before their eyes and giving them one last chance to avoid complete heartbreak. He wants to make these women feel devastation. To be deprived of someone that they really wanted. I think that if any of these women had said 'yes' to his proposals that he'd have just disappeared into the wind. Killing these men is his way of working his way up to killing someone he's been raging against for a long time. He said to Chip Walker that he didn't kill women. Not yet, but I think that's where he's heading."

"We're going to interview Mary Brennen to see who she may have been serious with while attending college before she got engaged to Kevin Berkley," McClure said.

"Yes," Etheridge said. "I don't have to tell you to be very thorough with that interview, Jared. The individual you're after could have been a student there, and she may have met him or even dated him. If her story matches the story of Anne Scarborough and Kim Montgomery, and better yet, supplies you with a name, then you may find your man, depending upon what she gives you. She herself could be at risk of injury or harm if this guy was scamming her like the other women."

"Where do you think his home base might be?" Kenny Smith asked.

"His first victim was a college student at UVA. My guess is that his home base is Virginia. One of the women said that his car had Virginia plates and that his driver's license was issued in Virginia. He's probably living within the Richmond metro area. I think that the location of the cyber café where he set up his false social media profiles is a small and subtle digital "tell" on his part. His attempted murder on the Outer Banks failed. He's not used to failure. He'll return to more familiar surroundings in order to rethink his calculus going forward. Listen all, I have another meeting that I need to get ready for. Good hunting gents, and I'll be in touch about that fishing trip, Marty. And of course, please call me if you get this guy?"

121

"Will do," Tate said. The other officers said their thank you and goodbyes and McClure disconnected the call.

"Thanks for putting this guy in the loop, Marty," McClure said.

"My pleasure," Tate said. "I hope that Bill's description of this monster that we're chasing will help to strengthen your interview with Ms. Brennen, depending on what she tells you."

"It will," McClure said. He reached across the table and picked up the police artist sketch of David Wiggins. He studied it and then looked around the table at the other three uniformed men.

"It will," he said again. "Because after listening to Bill, my gut tells me that there's a strong probability that she dated this guy, and thus she became the first victim of his fantasy game."

"Me too," Tate said.

Fred Drury and Kenny Smith agreed as well.

"And just maybe," McClure said. "Just maybe, we'll get his real name."

"You're thinking that he changed it to David Wiggins after he killed Kevin Berkley?" Kenny Smith asked.

"Yes," McClure said. "A new identity to use in his new hunting grounds of the Outer Banks."

Chapter 21

Kenny Smith headed back to the Outer Banks and Marty Tate diverted to Williamsburg to spend the night and to enjoy dinner with his son. They decided to meet at The Red Talon, and once more, Marty looked forward to treating them both to a great meal. Tate was also anxious to hear some news about a part-time interpreter job that he had taken with the Colonial Williamsburg Foundation.

They met outside the front door and once inside the hostess seated them at a table that was opposite the bar. Robert stuffed his backpack, which was full of textbooks, on a nearby chair and Marty slid a tin box across the table.

"What's inside?" Robert asked his father.

"Your mom's homemade tollhouse cookies," Marty said with a grin on his face.

Robert picked up the tin and shook it.

"I'll bet this box is lighter than when you left home with it," Robert said with a smile. "How many did you have with your cups of coffee?"

"I only ate six. There's a dozen and a half more in there," Marty said with a smile as he pointed at the box with his large right index finger.

"So... I should be happy that there's any left at *all*, is that it?" Robert said.

"Damn straight," Marty said. "I'm hungry. Let's order?"

They each enjoyed starter plates of Prince Edward Island mussels served with wedges of garlic toast. For the main dishes, Marty had a grilled steak and Robert had a loaded burger and fries. Robert drank iced tea and Marty had a cold Bud Light. While they ate, they exchanged pleasant conversation.

"So what's this new job that you've taken up?" Marty asked his son.

"I'm proud to announce that beginning next weekend, I will be a firearms interpreter at the Historic Area's Magazine," Robert said.

"The tall, brick octagonal tower that stands just off of D.O.G. Street?"

"Yep," Robert said with a smile.

Tate held up his right hand in a high-five gesture and Robert shot out his right hand to meet his father's.

"Congratulations, son." Marty said.

The Magazine was built in 1715 by Governor Spotswood, and it stored equipment and weapons necessary for protection against possible Indian raids, slave revolts, riots and/or pirate raids. Later events at the Magazine in 1775 mirrored the events of the American Revolution that were taking place in Massachusetts. "D.O.G. Street," was the affectionate nickname given by the local population for the Duke of Gloucester Street.

"What will your new job entail?" Marty asked.

"I'll be stationed inside the Magazine and I'll be demonstrating the various weapons that were common during the time of the Revolution. Things like bayonets and muskets and rifles. And, I get to dress up in Colonial Militia attire," Robert said.

There was a waiting line now formed at the front door of the restaurant, and the eager diners in line scoped out the place like hovering buzzards in search of fresh road kill. The space was loud with conversation and laughter, and the sounds of glasses being clinked and knives and forks scraping tableware. Marty ordered a second round of drinks for himself and his son.

"So, let me get this straight," Marty said. "You found someone to pay you to engage in one of your favorite hobbies?"

Robert nodded. He was taught by his father at the age of 14 how to safely load and discharge a variety of firearms. When he was of age, Marty would take him to the firing range, and Robert developed into a marksman. He and Marty also enjoyed hunting Eastern Wild Turkeys in the fall.

"After my orientation there, my supervisor said that I could transfer over to the new, outdoor musket firing range and serve as an instructor to the tourists."

"I'm impressed but not surprised," Marty said. "Good for you, son."

"Thanks, Dad. But at least I don't have to worry about targets that return fire. What brings you back to Virginia so soon? Not that I'm complaining."

"The same case that I told you about when I was here last. The perpetrator that we're after recently made a run at a friend of mine back home."

"Oh my God… Is your friend alright?"

"Yes," Marty said. "But he was smart and lucky enough to get away. Earlier today, I was up near C'Ville on a conference call with the FBI and the Virginia State Police."

"This guy sounds dangerous," Robert said.

"He is. And he's smart and elusive," Marty said as he took a pull on his Bud Light bottle.

"As dangerous as the guy that you had to shoot and kill last year? Mark Lonsway?"

"I'd say so," Marty said as he looked directly into his son's eyes.

"Your job demands more courage than I think that I could muster up, Dad."

"It doesn't mean that I'm not scared when I have to draw my service weapon," Marty said. He looked around the room as he and Robert waited for their cider poached apple pastry desserts. He took a final swig of his beverage and looked back at his son across the table.

"To quote a famous and courageous man," Tate said.

"'Courage is not the absence of fear, but rather the assessment that something else is more important than fear.'"

Robert pursed his lips and studied his father's face as he contemplated the original owner of the quote.

"Okay, I give up," Robert said. "Who said it?"

Marty smiled.

"I'll give you a hint. He was the youngest Assistant Secretary of the Navy before he became President, and his fifth cousin once-removed held the same post and also became an American President."

"FDR," Robert said as he shook his head and held up his glass of iced tea in a gesture of admiration. "It took a lot of courage to fight polio."

"It did," Marty said.

"But as far as I know, FDR never had to shoot someone in the line of service and never got wounded in close combat, like you were last year."

"True, but the answer to what I did out on that stormy beach last year is in FDR's quote. I *was* afraid. But, preserving lives was more important than my fear. So I reacted to the situation, and followed my training, and it was over in the blink of an eye. My gunshot wound healed. FDR had to struggle with the pains of polio every damned day."

"I'm glad that you're here, Dad. Stay safe on the job for all of us, okay?"

"Always," Marty said, beholding his son and thinking also of his wife and daughter.

Their desserts arrived, and after a while, the restaurant's crowd thinned out. They walked outside and decided to take a night - time stroll as far as the Magazine, and studied the historic structure under the full moon sky before it was time for Robert to get back to his dorm, and for Marty to get some sleep before he took on an early drive back to the Outer Banks.

* * * * *

That same August evening found Richard Dolenz inside his one bedroom warehouse apartment in Richmond, Virginia, just a few blocks away from the James River. He held his phone up to his ear as he studied his reflection in the window that looked out over the street below. On the third ring, his call was answered.

"Why, hello Richard," Julia Dolenz said from her home in Williamsburg. "I haven't heard from you in ages. You must be in some sort of money trouble."

Her son took in a long breath of air in order to control his anger. He always became angry when his mother was right. Or even when she wasn't.

"Hello, mother," he replied as calmly as he could. "And I'm not in any money trouble. Not yet, anyway. But I soon will be if you don't restore my full allowance."

"Ah. That's what this call is about. Hold the line won't you? I just remembered something." She held her phone away from her ear and shouted some instructions into the room where she was standing.

Richard listened as Julia called out to a Cordelia, asking her to make dinner reservations for herself and Reggie tomorrow night, then she returned to their call.

"So sorry about that," she said.

"I didn't know that you had someone there. Have you hired a secretary?" he asked.

"Oh I was just speaking to my electronic administrative assistant. Everyone seems to have one now. I call her Cordelia. It's made by a new company called Timespan. She's almost like having a real assistant. She makes my life so efficient. So tell me. How are you getting on, Richard? You should come to Williamsburg to meet Reggie. He's only seen your picture."

"Perhaps if you restore my full allowance, I'd be able to afford treating the three of us to a handsome meal. I'll have to defer until I get some more photography work," he said.

"All of that fine, expensive education that I paid for and you're still just snapping pictures," she said. "You need to invest your time in a proper living, Richard. Why don't you consider being a real journalist?"

"In case you've missed it, mum, the internet is replacing printed newspapers. Newspaper outlets are sacking writers, they're not hiring them. But they still do pay for pictures as you call them."

"I suppose that you have a point. So, why don't you pop down for a visit?"

"Why don't you return my full allowance?"

"I've already told you, Richard. Money is being set aside in a trust account for you. I haven't disowned you. I daresay that you'll inherit a right tidy sum after I've passed away. In the meantime, you'll have to make do with what you earn, just like the rest of us."

"You're living off of the inheritance that Father left you. You haven't had to work a day in your life after you married him. My one bedroom flat here in Richmond costs over a thousand quid a month, and the lease on my car isn't cheap either. It's a wonder I can afford to eat."

"Are you quite through ranting? If those last remarks were designed to get me to change my mind about your allowance, well..." she drifted off.

He listened for her next comments but none came. He decided to change gears a bit.

"How about restoring three fourths of my allowance? Father would want me to have that money."

"That would turn out to be a slippery slope for my pocketbook, Richard. And now, you're trying to play the guilt card

127

with me. It won't work. Your father's wishes were quite clear. He instructed me in words as well as in his last will and testament that I was to decide how money was to be spent - or given - to you. So, leave the poor man's memory out of this. I'm the decider. Get yourself into a higher paying occupation. Find a more modest apartment. Lease a less expensive car. Do those things, then *perhaps* I'll reconsider."

"But don't you want me to be happy?"

"Yes," Julia said. "As well as fiscally responsible. Now, the evening is getting on and I have other things to do before bedtime. Goodnight, Richard," she said as she rang off.

"*Bitch*," he hissed into the disconnected phone. He walked over to the refrigerator and took out a bottle of cheap American beer, unscrewed the cap, and sat down in the kitchen to mull things over.

Chapter 22

The next day at lunchtime, Jared McClure and Fred Drury were seated under a red umbrella in the outdoor dining space of the popular C'Ville Burger Bar on Main Street in downtown Charlottesville. They had ordered iced tea and were waiting for Mary Brennen who worked as an assistant manager of a long established bookstore just a few blocks away. McClure had sent a picture of himself and Trooper Drury to her cell phone so that she would recognize them easily, although they were both in uniform and stood out in the crowd. The place was packed as usual.

As the iced teas were delivered, Fred Drury looked over McClure's shoulder and returned a wave to the attractive young woman who was approaching the table. McClure turned around. He assessed her height to be 5' 8" tall. Her hair was auburn and fell loosely about her shoulders. She made a small wave again when she noticed that McClure had spotted her. The two men rose from the table to greet her.

"Good afternoon, Ms. Brennen," McClure said as he held out his hand. She shook it.

"Good afternoon, Lt. McClure," she said. "Please call me Mary."

"Yes ma'am," McClure said and next he introduced her to Trooper Fred Drury.

McClure paid for the iced teas, and both men donned their black straw campaign hats as they walked away from the restaurant.

"Are you familiar with Justice Park, Mary?" McClure asked.

"Oh yes," she replied. "It's one of my favorite places to have lunch, and it's only two blocks away."

"I hope that we're not intruding on your lunch break?" Drury said.

"Oh no. I had a sandwich at the bookstore before I left to come see you," she said.

They rounded the corner and beheld the tall, imposing statue of Thomas "Stonewall" Jackson atop his horse in full charge during the Civil War. The three found an empty park bench and sat a moment as people of both sexes walked their dogs or played Frisbee.

Two young mothers walked together in conversation with one another as they pushed their strollers down a path.

"Thank you for seeing us, Mary," McClure began. "You'll recall that weeks ago I had the unfortunate duty to notify you that we had discovered Kevin's remains in the Shenandoah National Park."

She looked at him and nodded.

"I'll never forget that call. You told me that Kevin had been killed. His family decided to have his remains cremated. I was invited to scatter them about the campus grounds of the University, a place that he and I both loved. It's where we met. It's where we were going to be married. At the Colonnade Club, right in the midst of the historic grounds."

"Once again," McClure said. "We're very sorry. We don't wish to distress you further. Fred and I are in charge of Kevin's homicide investigation. We have a few questions, if you'd be good enough to tell us what you can?"

"What kinds of questions?" She said. She had a look of distress on her youthful face.

"Not to worry, Mary. Many of the questions that the police had during Kevin's disappearance have already been answered by you. You were always in the clear of suspicion. That remains today. We're after a man that we think may have committed this awful deed. We believe that this man is the same man who killed a psychologist in North Carolina a couple of months back, and most recently tried to kill another man there."

"Oh my God," she said as she held up her right hand to her mouth. Based on his long career of interviewing subjects, McClure thought that the distress on her face appeared to be morphing into shock.

"How was the other man killed?" Mary asked.

"He died of a gunshot wound most likely from a handgun," Drury answered in a neutral tone. "The recent assault also involved a handgun."

"But as I told the police a year ago, Kevin had no enemies. What makes you both think that this is the same man?"

"We have physical evidence as well as leads that we're pursuing. We're coordinating our investigation with the Sheriff of Dare County in North Carolina. We've taken what we've learned to

130

the FBI. With luck and persistence, we hope to apprehend this offender and bring him to justice." McClure said.

She nodded then looked in the direction of where a dog was chasing a tennis ball.

"Essentially, we need to ask you if you had any other serious relationships during your college years before you met Kevin," Drury said.

She looked at Drury. He noted a tincture of confusion in her eyes.

"No. Nothing serious. Of course I dated some other people. Ideas about marriage no doubt were discussed, but, there was no one else for me but Kevin. He was my one and only. It's been over a year and I haven't returned to dating."

McClure sensed a growing tension and eased out another question.

"No man proposed marriage to you while you were in college besides Kevin? Is that correct?"

Silence. She looked away at some pigeons that were walking their way towards them.

"No," she said. "I mean… That's correct. Just Kevin." She continued to look at the pigeons.

McClure looked over to Fred Drury. Fred nodded his head slightly before he withdrew a letter-sized piece of paper from the inside pocket of his tunic. He handed it over to McClure. McClure opened it to reveal the police artist sketch of the so-called "David Wiggins."

"Mary, would you please look at this sketch made by a police artist and tell me if you've ever seen this man before?" McClure said as he handed her the sketch.

She looked back up at him and nodded and took the sketch in her hands. When she looked down at it, McClure noted that she raised her eyebrows and her eyes widened in what his many years of training and experience told him was a sign of recognition. Slowly, she started to shake her head and held the paper away from her as if it were a rancid piece of food that disgusted her. McClure retrieved the paper from her hands.

"No," she finally said. "I've never seen that guy. Is he the one that you suspect killed Kevin?"

"Yes," McClure said.

She wrapped her arms around herself and shivered in the sunny eighty degree Northern Virginia summer air. The pigeons had moved on, but she was looking down at the spot where they last were.

McClure cast his eyes over to Drury who gave him a slight head nod. He had assessed her reaction to the sketch as well.

"You're absolutely positive that you've never seen this man before?" McClure asked her.

"Yes, I'm sure, Lieutenant," she said. "It's been a little over a year since Kevin died. I mean… since he was killed. While I'm coming to terms with that, you'll have to understand that this is a very difficult time for me and for the members of his family. And I certainly don't want to revisit my past before Kevin."

She looked back up at him. He nodded at her. Pushing back the emotional waves of disappointment that were running through his bloodstream, he reached inside his tunic and presented her with his official state police business card.

"Mary, if you can recall anyone that may have wished Kevin harm last year, please don't hesitate to call me personally."

She accepted the card and then she stood up. The two men did likewise.

"I'm sorry that I can't help you." She said. "I have to be getting back to the store now. I hope that you catch whoever did this to Kevin."

She turned from them abruptly and then turned a corner at a quickstep and was out of view.

"*Damn* it," Drury said.

"Yep," said McClure.

"She knows the guy in the sketch," Drury said.

"Yep."

"Her cutting off the interview just now seems to confirm that, doesn't it?"

"Yep," McClure said looking in the direction of where she disappeared into the crowd.

"We're not going to follow her back to her store?"

"Nope."

"*Damn* it!"

"Yep."

"Do you think she's covering for the David Wiggins guy who's in the sketch?"

"Nope," McClure said as he started walking out of the park.

"I think that she knows who the guy is and she isn't saying anything because she's either quite shocked that he could be capable of murdering Kevin or she's forcefully blocked the memories of the past. Or, after seeing the sketch and hearing our story, she doesn't want to get involved."

"Shit," Drury said as they both continued walking.

"I'll give her a few days, then I'll call her back to see how she's doing. Maybe the thought of seeing justice done for Kevin's sake will outweigh her shock or concerns and she'll tell me what she knows about the man in the sketch. Other than that, we can't keep calling her or showing up at her apartment or her place of business."

"Because that would be police harassment," Drury said.

"Yep."

"*Damn* it," Drury said yet again as they made their way back to their service vehicle which was illegally parked on Main Street.

Chapter 23

Two evenings later, Terry Grant was prowling the streets of
Williamsburg masquerading as a pizza deliveryman. He had on a
navy blue cotton shirt and wore a four buttoned opened denim vest
over jeans and low top sneakers. On his head he wore a black
colonial tricorn hat and he carried an empty cardboard pizza box also
designed with three corners. The words, "Tricorn Pizzeria" were
stenciled on the box top. The costume as well as the oddly-shaped
pizza were all a part of the schtick at the popular pizza joint which
was located near The College of William and Mary. To complete the
disguise, he wore a black eye mask, much like the character *Zorro*
used to wear in the classic old movies. The navy backpack that he
carried contained all of the essential tools which were required to
carry out tonight's skullduggery, or as others would call it, sheer
madness.

With a little time on his hands, he strolled past the Merchants
Square Ticket Office on Henry Street where out-of-town tourists
stood in a long line. They were there he supposed in order to
purchase their overpriced admittance to tonight's guided Tavern
Ghost Walk, a popular evening program during which a colonial-
costumed, lantern-carrying interpreter would lead the guileless
tourists around the various historical taverns such as The Raleigh,
The King's Arms, and Shields to name just a few. At each stop, the
interpreter would fill their heads and tickle their spines with ghoulish
tales of the tormented ghosts that haunted the old buildings at night
in numbers as thick as thieves.

"*Rubbish,*" Terry said as he strolled past the ticket office
before he doubled back and headed for Francis Street and the law
offices of Reginald White et al.

Returning his thoughts to the matter at hand, tonight's
dishonorable proceedings were going to be carried out like a brilliant
thespian performance that had been scrupulously planned and well-
rehearsed. He had even taken the precaution of removing the SIM
card from his phone, making his movements and location impossible
to track. He had calculated that it was time to get off the grid until
the oncoming shit storm passed away. Over the past days he had

choreographed a terrific and terrifying final scene for his clueless victim. This was to be a cold-blooded act of mortal stakes. Indeed, tonight's macabre tragedy should prove to be more shocking to his prey than a scene portrayed on a creepy old Alfred Hitchcock movie like several that he and his mum used to watch on the telly back home. Because this was real. This was for keeps.

"Jeepers, creepers. *Scarrry* shit, boys and girls," he said out loud to no one before he cackled to himself along the dark, near-empty street, spinning the empty pizza box in his hands. Tonight he would settle a score. He would remove a malignant growth in human form who was fucking everything up.

Terry Grant was here to make things right. To return everything to as it was in the past. And, once he crossed the threshold of the law office, there would be no going back. No second guessing. No pity. No hesitation. No remorse. *No sir.* Terry had done all of his meticulous homework and had reasoned the outcome and consequences of his actions to his complete satisfaction. And everything made smashing sense inside of that beautiful mind of his.

He reached the front door of the law office and scanned the surroundings. All was quiet as it should be at nine o'clock at night on this summer evening. Across the street on the corner streetlamp post a sign reading: "Warning! Neighborhood Crime Watch. We Report All Suspicious Persons and Activities To Law Enforcement." He grinned broadly as he briefly considered the irony of the sign's location. The parking lot across the street where his expensive car was parked was nearly deserted. He knew about the surveillance camera that was mounted three feet over his head. He also knew that Reginald White would be alone in his office thanks to spoofing the phone of Julia Dolenz. How nice of Richard to provide Terry with Mumsie's phone number. It was time to make his play. He pushed the buzzer next to the highly polished mahogany door and spoke into the speaker mounted next to the buzzer.

"Tricorn Pizzeria," he said, with a slight drawl, sounding like a genuine southerner. Yes sir, just like a born and bred citizen of the Old Dominion state.

Inside his office, Reggie White was indeed all alone in the building. He had been concentrating on the papers in front of him, which told the tale of an ugly and expensive drawn-out divorce, when he heard the buzzer and the announcement from the call box.

Reluctantly, he got up from his expensive desk and opened the door of his office which led out to the lobby. He leaned down over his assistant Linda's desk to look at the security monitor. A tall masked man wearing a silly costume holding a box was looking up and down as he chewed on what looked to be a large wad of bubblegum. He pushed the speaker button at the desk.

"I say," he said. "I didn't order any pizza. You must be mistaken."

The pizza delivery guy returned his gaze to the outside call box and replied.

"I didn't say that you ordered it, sir. We got a call from (757) 237 - 8529. The caller's name was Miss Linda Bell. She says I was to deliver this here pizza to a Mr. Reggie White who was working late and might like something to eat. So, here I am, pal."

Reggie recognized his assistant's name as well as the number of the law office which spelled out "Best Law." Linda had performed this kind of thoughtfulness in the past but she usually checked with him first. She usually avoided surprising him, especially when she knew he was looking over a complex case. He spoke back to the pizza guy.

"I'm afraid that you must be the victim of some kind of hoax. It's not like Linda to order something without checking with me first."

"You Mr. White?" The deliveryman said.

"Yes. Yes, that's right. I am the founder of the law firm, and I need to get back to a matter that requires my strict attention, so I will bid you a good evening, sir."

"Hold on, pal," the deliveryman replied sounding irritated. "If you don't do the decent thing and pay me for this grease slice, my boss back at the Pizzeria will take it out of my pay. I don't have a lot of money like you wealthy lawyers do. Docking me for a pizza and a tip puts a big hit on a college student's income, if you dig what I'm sayin'? Y' all know what I mean, *pal?*"

"Oh, alright then. Exactly how much for the pizza?" Reggie said.

"Twelve dollars for the large pepperoni slice... Plus *tip*," the deliveryman replied.

"Hold on then and let me get some petty cash," Reggie said. *What a brash and annoying nuisance,* Reggie thought as he opened one of the drawers of a nearby desk and retrieved a twenty dollar bill.

"Yes sir," the deliveryman said respectfully as he turned his back to the front door.

Things are going swimmingly, Terry thought to himself as he grinned from ear to ear before he spit out his wad of chewing gum. He removed a weapon from out of his backpack and held it in his right hand under the pizza box that he held like a serving tray in his left. He heard the door open and he spun around. *And away we go!* He thought to himself.

Reginald White, esquire, beheld the male figure who stood before him. He was about his own height and the figure beamed a perverted grin across his face. Despite the eye mask that the uninvited deliveryman was wearing, Reginald thought for a moment that his eyes appeared crazed. He looked down and studied the open vest and the strange, tricorn - shaped box, and next he noticed the menacing black and yellow Taser that the strange man was pointing at him. Before he could utter a sound, two small dart - like electrodes carrying 50,000 volts of unpleasantness hit him in his chest. His knees buckled and then he hit the wooden floor of the office in a state of neuromuscular incapacitation. He wanted to retaliate against his attacker, but the darts had disrupted the voluntary control of his muscles. He was temporarily helpless.

Terry tossed the pizza box across the floor and withdrew a pair of plastic handcuffs from his backpack and strapped Reggie's hands together at his wrists. He put on a pair of latex gloves and he closed the door behind him and locked it. He removed the darts from White's chest which were still connected to the Taser by wires. He replaced the Taser in his backpack with a black .22 caliber Browning Buckmark semi - automatic pistol with a suppressor attached to the end of the barrel.

"Let's get on with this, shan't we?" Terry said without the phony accent as he took off his tricorn hat and grabbed Reggie White by the opened collar of his shirt. Reggie was wearing one of his favorite ties loosely about his neck, and now it was strangling him as he was hoisted to his feet by the strong intruder.

"Let's use your office for this visit," Terry said as he dragged along his victim who was staggering like a drunken sailor before Grant stuffed him in his expensive red leather chair behind his desk.

"Who are you?" Reggie demanded slurring his speech.

Terry sat opposite him inside one of the expensive client chairs, holding the pistol as he crossed his arms in front of him.

"I'm Death," Terry said as he slowly waved the pistol in front of Reggie's face. "I'm Death on two bloody legs, as a matter of fact. I already *know* who you are. Now that we've been formally introduced, is there anything that you care to say before I put a bullet in that thick skull of yours?"

His voice sounded calm and businesslike. Professional. Like an unenthusiastic server asking a patron for their dinner order. Like he didn't give a fuck or a rat's ass about the doomed man's reply.

Reggie cleared his throat before he answered. He lifted up his bound hands and loosened the tie around his neck.

"Why are you assaulting me? Are you some disgruntled former client? If you are I could give you a very handsome sum of money if you promise to go away. I mean, why *on earth* would you wish to kill me?"

"This interview is growing rather tedious, don't you think?" Terry said. "I'm going to kill you because *she* said, 'No.'"

"Who's '*she*'?" Reginald White asked in disbelief.

"Why, *Julia*, of course," Terry said before he removed his eye mask from his face with his left hand. Next, he racked the slide on the semi-automatic as it pointed towards the ceiling before he leveled it and pointed the barrel between Reggie's eyes.

"YOU!" He gasped with an astonished look on his face and shock in his voice.

"Of course," Terry said, before he pulled the trigger and instantly ended the rich lawyer's life on earth. The impact of the bullet forced Reginald White's body to catapult up and back in his chair before gravity forced his lifeless torso to fall flat on his face on the surface of his old desk, his blood spattered over the legal paperwork.

"There," Terry said. "No more chit chat."

He put the gun in his backpack and removed a brand new pair of very sharp pruning shears whose incisors gleamed under the office light. He leaned over the desk and grabbed Reggie White's bound hands which were sprawled above his head and took the left hand in his and then he harvested the dead man's wedding ring finger.

138

"You shan't be needing this anymore, my good man," Terry said as he mocked his lifeless victim. He placed the severed digit inside a small plastic bag and stuffed it in the backpack.

He walked back to the lobby and replaced the mask over his eyes and placed the tricorn hat on his head. He could hear the ticking of the large grandfather clock that stood in the corner of the lobby. He heard the ringing of a cell phone coming from the dead lawyer's office.

"I'll bet I know who's trying to get a hold of *you*, Reggie! Boooo – hoo," he said out loud as he walked over to the assistant's desk and took a seat. He opened a wooden panel near his left leg and found what he was looking for. It was the control panel for the surveillance camera. He found the button that he was looking for and erased the past 24 hour history from the camera outside and shut down the system.

Content that he had everything that belonged to him tucked away in his backpack, he turned towards the front door and left quietly. His back was to the office the whole time that he walked across the street to his car. He got in, closed the door and removed his hat. He powered the car on and piloted the vehicle down the darkened South Boundary Street where he pulled over, removed his mask, and got out of the car to replace the rear license plate on the vehicle. Then he got back inside and headed south, bound for Nags Head, N.C... He was safely back in the wind.

"Freeway, cars and trucks," he sang along with the music on the radio to a few words from one of his favorite retro band Eagles' songs. He looked through the windshield out into the dark Virginia night as he cruised along obeying the speed limit on Interstate 64.

Every fiber of her being told her that something was dreadfully wrong. Julia Dolenz parked her car across from the law office and got out calling Reggie's mobile phone for the third time in the last 30 minutes. Once again, she got no reply. It was nearly midnight. Reggie should have been at her house by no later than 11:00pm. He hadn't called to say that he was working later than expected. Julia had found him to be as dependable as the tide and taxes, which was one of his character traits that she most admired. She used her pass key to open the door of the law office and stepped inside.

"Reggie?" She called out, but all was still except for the ticking of the grand old clock that stood in the corner. She walked closer to the receptionist's desk and down and to her right, laying atop the wooden floor was a triangular - shaped box. She leaned down and picked it up. When she turned it over she saw the words, "Tricorn Pizzeria" stenciled on top. She opened it. It was empty. She smelled the box and there was no residual odor. It was just an empty box.

"How rather queer," she said out loud in a soft voice.

She set the box down atop the receptionist's desk and made her way to Reggie's office. Just outside his office door she detected an odor that she was very familiar with. Gunpowder.

"NO!" Julia said as she stepped inside the threshold and sighted Reggie's inert remains slumped over the top of his desk.

She wanted to scream. Instead, her right hand came up and covered her mouth. Tears welled-up in her eyes as she shook her head back and forth in disbelief.

"No, no, no," she said repeatedly as she walked cautiously and closer to the body. She knew that he was dead. She had been in the presence of death before. Her first husband's death was not altogether unexpected. Imperceptible to those around him, she knew privately that he was failing in health for a couple of days before the end. This was much different. This was a shocking, unforeseen loss that made absolutely no sense. She reached the desk and saw the spatters of blood on the paperwork that lay around and under her late fiancé's head. She gently took hold of his head and rolled it backwards until she could make out the small but fatal entry wound.

140

She replaced his head where it was and kissed him gently on his crown. Next, she noticed that Reggie's hands had been bound by a plastic strap at his wrists, before she next comprehended the bloody mutilation of his left hand.

Julia dug her cell phone out of her jacket in order to call the police. She pushed the preset number for 911, before a wave of nausea and dizziness overcame her. After she placed her call she sat down in one of the client chairs and put her head between her knees while she waited for the police.

My Good God, she thought. *Reggie inevitably made enemies in his work, but he's been in this business a long time, and he's never mentioned anything about receiving a credible death threat... Perhaps it might be prudent to consider another horrible possibility about who has done this wretched thing. A possibility that touches much closer to home...*

Chapter 24

The following morning, Richard Dolenz awoke with a headache following an unfit sleep. He walked barefoot into the bathroom, turned on the light and opened up the medicine cabinet and unscrewed the top of an aspirin bottle. He took out three capsules and swallowed them before he turned on the faucet and stuck his head underneath for a quick swallow of water. He groaned and looked at himself in the mirror.

"Fuck," he said aloud, dragging out the one syllable word as he let out his breath.

He stumbled his way to the kitchen and looked to his right. Through the bank of windows which faced the east he could make out the rising sun as well as the outline of a man sitting quietly in a high-back chair. From the familiar outline of his head Richard knew that it was Terry, and he relaxed as he made his way to the island counter and started preparing coffee.

"Good morning, mate. Would you care for some coffee?" Richard called out.

"You've been asking me that question for what seems like centuries, Richard, and the answer is always the same."

"I know. I know. You don't need coffee. I get it. Suit yourself because I'm having some," Richard said.

"No doubt you need it," he heard Terry say. "I noticed that you drank the head and shoulders of that bottle of bourbon that I saw in the kitchen."

Richard looked over to the cabinet where he kept the booze and saw the bottle on the counter just as Terry had described.

"I'm surprised that I didn't have more, the way that I'm feeling," Richard said.

Terry Grant turned round in his chair and looked across the room to look at Richard. Richard perceived the grin on his familiar face.

"Oh ye of little faith," Terry said. "Everything will shine brighter by tomorrow morning I should think. You forget that things always work out in your favor in the end, old boy."

Richard nodded at him. The coffee maker made a beeping sound announcing that the java was ready.

He took a mug out of the cabinet in front of him and poured himself a cup. He took a swig and found it to be satisfyingly delicious.

"Don't you remember that beastly bully of a boy who used to rough you up back in the eighth grade? You kept asking him to stop, but he wouldn't."

"Sean O'Casey?" Richard said.

"That's right," Terry said. "Then along came one glorious day and little shitbag Sean O'Casey got run over by a car on Henry Street whilst he was riding his bike in Williamsburg. The fat bully snot got what was coming to him if you ask me," Terry said.

Richard nodded.

"And then there was that bloke in high school who stole your girl when you were a senior. You had really fallen head over heels for her, I daresay. She most certainly had a fine looking, first - rate ass. I recall that her name was Maureen... Anyway, where was I going with this?"

"You're about to remind me that Clive McDonald - that was the name of the bloke who stole Maureen - got killed in a car accident right before our graduation."

"That's right," Terry said. "The wanker voted "Most Likely to Succeed" tore out of the parking lot of the high school in his brand new, high powered, hot shit car that his fucking parents had bought for him, and he drove right into the back end of a semi-trailer. High five for Clive! He's no longer alive! Cheerio! Good night and good riddance," Terry said as he waved his hand in the air mockingly and with much enthusiasm.

Richard grinned as he recalled the memory.

"And just over a year ago, Mary Brennen threw you over for that Kevin Berkley chap. She said that she loved you, but you knew that she was a lying whore. What she really loved was Kevin's family's money, the greedy, self-centered gold digger slut. Still, you had asked her - hell - you *begged* her to reconsider, but she said, 'no.' Don't you remember how depressed and humiliated you were?" Terry said.

"Whatever happened to him? To that Kevin Berkley chap?" Richard said.

He looked over at Terry who made a gesture with his hands and arms as if he were sculpting an image of a nuclear mushroom cloud from the floor up to the ceiling.

"Poof," Terry said. "No more Kevin. Kevin hasn't phoned home. No one's heard from Kevin in over a year. Kevin just disappeared. Poof." He made the gesture again.

"Perhaps he found a new conquest? Someone just as good looking but richer than Mary and her bloody family," Richard postulated. There was no reply from Terry.

"Face it," Terry eventually said. "When people get on the bad side of you it's as if they develop some form of dreadful karma that eventually spells doom for them. Don't worry. Things will look brighter in the morning."

"So you said," Richard said. "How do *you* know?"

Terry hiked his shoulders and cocked his head.

"You'll see," he said.

"So you say," Richard said as he retreated to the bathroom to ingest a few more aspirins. They'd make his stomach feel like shit but his head would feel a whole lot better. He opened the bottle and swallowed two more aspirins.

When he returned to the kitchen, he looked out towards the living room window. The sun was riding higher in the clear summer sky as it shone through the apartment window casting a bright, trapezoidal patterned glow on the wooden floors. And Terry Grant was gone.

Chapter 25

Marty Tate was sitting behind his desk in his office in Manteo reading a number of reports about burglaries in the town of Duck when Peggie appeared at his door.

"There's a pretty young woman here to see you, Martin," she said.

"How pretty?" he said.

"See for yourself if you can make time for her? She said it's important. Her name is Kim Montgomery."

Tate put down the report he was reading and pursed his lips.

"Please show her in," he said.

He stood up and in a moment Kim Montgomery walked in, carrying her electronic notepad.

"I'm sorry to bother you, Sheriff," she said. "But I came across something late last night that you should see."

"It's quite alright. Please take a seat." Tate said.

Kim seated herself across from Tate.

"Have you gotten rid of that phone that you told us about? The one that David Wiggins gave you?"

"I did. As soon as you told me how it could be used. I had already changed my phone number at Megan Treadwell's suggestion, but..." Her voice trailed off. She continued.

"You see, late last night I was scrolling around the internet shopping for wedding photographers, and I found one named Sea Side Wedding Photography. I liked some of the pictures that were displayed on the home page, so I started to learn more about them under their 'About Us' tab. May I show you what I found?"

Tate wore a serious expression on his face as Kim Montgomery stood up and came around his desk and put her notebook down on the desk in front of him. He looked down at what appeared to be the home page for Sea Side Wedding Photography. Several photos of couples getting married on the beach were displayed.

"Take a look under the tab labeled, 'About Us,'" she said.

He looked up at her.

"How do I work this thing?"

"Just use your index finger. It'll go where you point it, just like a smart phone," she said.

Tate looked back down at the machine and moved his large right index finger around the screen. He put his finger on the website's 'About Us' tab and the screen now showed what must be a brief history of the company as well as the picture of a man who bore a strong and utterly remarkable resemblance to the police sketch that he had shown to Kim and Chip. The unknown subject who had killed two men and tried to kill a third. The unknown subject with the phony name.

"Son of a bitch," he said as he studied the man's face and features.

"Now you understand why I had to see you this morning," she said. "*That's* the man who called himself David Wiggins. I'm *positive* of this. I rocked back in my chair when I first saw his picture last night. But his name isn't David Wiggins on this website. It's something else entirely." She pointed at the screen.

"Richard Dolenz," Tate said out loud. "The business is based out of Richmond, Virginia."

"It's him," Kim said. "That's the man I dated and the same man that tried to kill Chip. Can you go after him?"

Tate turned his head upward and met her look.

"I can and I will," he said. "And with the help of the Virginia State Police. It looks as if you've caught us quite a break. Thanks, Kim. We may never have found this if you weren't getting married to Chip."

He reached out his hand and she shook it. She reached down and retrieved her notebook and started for the door. She paused and looked back at him.

"Thank you, Sheriff Tate. If you can get this man in a line-up, I'm certain that I could positively identify him, especially if I heard his voice to go along with his face."

"We'll see if that can be arranged. Thanks again, Kim, and give my best to Chip?"

She nodded and smiled, then left the office. Tate paged Peggie.

"Peggie? Where's Kenny this morning?"

"He's at home. He's taking the late shift today, don't you remember?"

"Oh yeah. Thanks," Tate said as he reached for his phone. He hit the speed dial for Kenny Smith, and after a few rings he got an answer.

"Are you near your computer?" Tate asked. He waited.

"Now I am," Kenny Smith said as he sat in front of his home computer wearing an old sweat suit.

"Good. Now find a search engine and type in *Sea Side Wedding Photography*."

"I've got it. Let me open up the website… Got it. Now what?"

"Shoot up to the banner and click the 'About Us' tab."

Tate listened carefully for a reaction.

"Son of a *bitch*," Kenny said. "That's our guy! The guy who calls himself, David Wiggins. It says here that his name is Richard Dolenz, with a business address in Richmond. Good work, Marty!"

"I wish that I could take the credit, but I can't. Kim Montgomery found this last night and brought it to me just a few minutes ago. She's positive that this is our guy. You're no longer working the late shift. Get dressed and get here as soon as you can."

"Will do. When are you going to call McClure?"

"After I hang up with you," Tate said.

* * * * *

That same morning, Lt. Jared McClure stood at his desk inside the Area 14 State Police office in Luray. He read a note that had a handwritten banner marked "Urgent." The message read: "Ron Kelso, Chief of the Williamsburg police department needs you to call him back as soon as possible." The phone number followed. He sat down and dialed the number. After a couple of rings there was an answer.

"Williamsburg Police. This is Brigid speaking. How may I help you?"

"Good morning, Brigid. This is Lt. Jared McClure of the state police returning Chief Kelso's call. Would you please patch me through to him?"

"Oh yes sir," she responded. "He's waiting for your call. I'll transfer you right over."

"Thanks," McClure said as he puzzled over the reason for the urgency. He took a seat behind his desk.

"Jared?" Ron Kelso said over the phone.

"Ron," Jared said. "It's been awhile. What's up?"

"A man was murdered down here last night execution – style."

"Okay," McClure said as he pulled out a pen from the top drawer of his desk.

"He was a successful attorney. Shot in the forehead while he sat at his office desk. The local medical examiner puts the time of death between 9 -10pm."

McClure noted this on a pad of paper.

"Okay," he said to Kelso again.

"You're wondering why I'm calling *you* about this," Kelso said.

"I know that you have a small force, Ron, but yeah, I'm curious."

"We scanned the ViCap database early this morning and found out that you and a Sheriff Martin Tate out of Manteo, North Carolina have active investigations underway for two different homicides that bear the same signature of this killer."

"Hold on. Are you telling me that your dead attorney is missing his wedding ring finger?" McClure said.

"That's right. Our local M.E. said that she feels that it was removed from his hand postmortem. Same as the other victims, right?"

"That's affirmative, Ron. Do you still have possession of his body?"

"Yep. We thought that you'd like to examine it before we send it over to the Office of the Chief Medical Examiner in Norfolk. We also have some surveillance footage from a nearby parking lot that you'll find interesting. How soon can you get down here?"

"About two hours without firing up the blue lights. I'd like to take Trooper Fred Drury along. He's familiar with the case. I'd also like to invite Sheriff Tate of he is available. He's also only two hours away from you."

"That'll be fine. The crime scene's locked down. How about if you and Trooper Drury and Sheriff Tate meet me here at my office and we can all go over there together?"

""That's fine. Two last things?"

"Shoot."

"What's the name of the victim and who reported it to you?"

"The victim's name is Reginald White. His fiancé' discovered his body when he failed to show up at her place by eleven last evening. She had your business card and has asked me to bring you in on this case."

"Her name?" McClure asked in puzzlement.

"By a sad coincidence, you've already met her, Jared. She was the semi-finalist at the charity shooting event in Newport News. She was the runner-up in the match."

"Julia Dolenz," McClure said as his mind raced back to the match. He remembered seeing her leave with a man after the trophies were awarded. He wondered now if the murder victim was the same man that he had seen.

"You should know that we don't like her for this homicide, Jared." Kelso said. "She had one of her girlfriends over at her house until about ten last night. The girlfriend's confirmed that. Ms. Dolenz has also given us her statement. I believe her."

"I don't like her for this either, Ron. She doesn't fit the profile that Sheriff Tate and I have put together. We're looking for a male offender for these homicides. And, I also heard you mention that your local M.E. put the time of the victim's death between nine and ten?"

"Okay," Kelso said. "I take it you'll be calling Sheriff Tate with an update when we're finished with this call?"

"Yeah, I'll be calling Marty. See you in a couple of hours, Ron," McClure said as they ended the call.

His next call was to the Dare County Sheriff's Office and Marty Tate. Peggie patched him through.

"Jared. I was just about to call *you*," Tate said.

"Oh?"

"Yeah. We may have gotten a huge break on the real identity of the character calling himself David Wiggins."

"That's good news, but I need to let you know that we had a homicide in Williamsburg last night. Not very far from the college campus."

"Jesus," Tate said as his mind flashed to the welfare of his son.

"I know. And I'm sure that your son is okay. The male victim was a lawyer and was shot execution-style in his office. His wedding ring finger is missing. Our guy's made another hit. So, what break have you got on this guy's real identity?"

"Ms. Kim Montgomery was here in my office this morning and she directed me to a website that she came across late last night of a wedding photographer that's based in Richmond. His picture is on his website. She's positive that it's our guy, and his picture is a dead ringer for the guy we have on the sketch that we've been showing around. The name listed on the website is Richard Dolenz."

McClure took an audible breath before he could respond.

"Marty, you and I have worked together long enough to know that neither you nor I like coincidences in a homicide investigation."

"Agreed. So, what *non* - coincidence are you talking about?" Tate said.

"Last night's murder victim? His body was discovered by his fiancé. Are you ready for this? Her name is Julia Dolenz."

"Sweet Jesus… A relative of this Richard character?"

"As sure as shit possible, I'd say. The Williamsburg police verified that Julia Dolenz has a solid alibi, and you and I both know that a woman isn't committing these murders. If Ms. Montgomery turns out to be right, she deserves a medal for this. I got nowhere with Mary Brennen. This smells like a *huge* non-coincidence to me. And to you too, I'm sure. How soon can you get up to Williamsburg P.D.? Ron Kelso, the chief, will meet us there."

"I'll have Peggie clear my schedule. I should be up there in about two hours. Let me have Kenny Smith ride along if you don't mind?"

"I don't mind at all. And keep your calendar wide open. If Ms. Dolenz identifies this Richard character as a relation of hers… say her son or a nephew for instance, then we'll be heading over to Richmond pronto."

"Copy that," Tate said. "See you in a couple of hours."

150

Chapter 26

Four hours later McClure, Drury, Tate and Smith were seated across from a Williamsburg police officer named Pete Langdon and Chief Kelso in a conference room, about to review last evening's surveillance footage of a Williamsburg parking lot. They had already gone over the crime scene and had viewed the victim's body. Williamsburg P.D. had pointed out the empty, oddly-shaped pizza box that they had collected as evidence at Reginald White's office. Kelso dimmed the lights of the conference room slightly and all present looked up at a projection screen where a black and white image that had been paused.

"Let me get to the right moment that we wanted you to see, gentlemen," Langdon said. He fast forwarded the frame a bit, found the time stamp that he was searching for, and clicked the button on his computer mouse.

The screen displayed a black and white image of a long row of cars parked in a line. Fortunately, the street lights were numerous and it made identification of the makes and models of the vehicles easy.

"Remember the empty tricorn shaped pizza box that we found inside the victim's office?" Kelso said to the investigators who all nodded their ascent.

"Well," Kelso continued. "The pizzeria has their delivery drivers wear colonial looking vests and tricorn hats when they are out on delivery."

"Okay," McClure said.

"Show them the footage, Pete," Kelso said.

Langdon hit the button on his computer mouse again and the law enforcement officers viewed a man with above average height and appearing to be slim in build wearing a vest and tricorn hat, carrying a backpack, entering the picture frame from the right side of the screen.

"One pizza deliveryman," Trooper Drury said.

"Yep," Kelso said. "And he's wearing a mask. We've looked at this several times and under magnification. His identity is hidden. He's walking from the direction of Mr. White's office. He's white, no mustache or beard, about six feet tall, and by the spring in his gait he *could* be college-aged. Now… watch where he goes." Kelso pointed his right index finger up at the screen.

The man without an identity strode deeper into the parking lot before he took something out of his pocket and pointed it. The rear lights of a brand new white BMW 5 Series blinked. The figure approached, opened the car's driver's side door and flung his backpack inside. Officer Langdon paused the playback.

"A white BMW… how about that?" Kenny Smith whispered to Marty Tate. Tate nodded.

"About how many pizza deliverymen would you suppose drive a new BMW 5 Series in this town?" Kelso said to the four invited investigators.

The four men looked at one another and shook their heads.

"Approximately *zero* would be our collective guess," Tate answered on their behalf.

"I'd concur," Kelso said. "Just to be sure, we asked the owner of the pizzeria to confirm this, and when we gave him the make and model of the car he said, 'You've got to be *shitting* me!' So, our mystery man doesn't work for Tricorn Pizzeria, but he disguised himself to look the part in order to gain entrance to Mr. White's law office with an empty pizza box. Mr. White must have let him in, as there were no signs of forced entry. As you saw back at the law office, the security footage from their front entrance has been scrubbed clean. We suspect that the offender knew how to do this and it was a part of his plan. We found the shell casing from the weapon - a .22 - but that's all that this guy left behind. No prints. A scrupulous and organized bastard, this one is. Okay, show them what comes next, Pete."

Langdon clicked on his mouse and the footage continued. The unidentified male with the odd hat got into the vehicle, closed the door and depressed the brake making the rear light bulbs glow. The reverse, back-up lights of the car were illuminated next, and the car eased out of its parking spot. The rear end of the car was now under the streetlamp and Officer Langdon paused the footage again.

"There," Langdon said as he pointed at the screen. "Do you all see it?"

The four investigators nodded. This time, McClure spoke for them.

"What we *don't* see... is a license plate," McClure said as he too pointed at the screen. Everyone nodded.

"Precisely," Chief Kelso said. "Like I said, this one's a careful and clever bastard. I'll give him that. He must have known that we'd find the surveillance footage from this parking lot, so he prepared for that eventuality. He wears his silly hat and mask the whole time that he's in the frame and has removed the plate from the expensive car, giving him almost total anonymity as he drives away. We've issued a B.O.L.O. on the car. I believe strongly that we're watching footage of Mr. Reginald White's murderer. Check out the date stamp of the footage - it reads: 10:30."

"I've already interviewed Julia Dolenz," Kelso said, looking across the table to the four men. "No doubt the both of you would like to speak with her as well?" Kelso said referring to McClure and Tate.

"We would," McClure said.

"She's keen on seeing you getting involved in this investigation, Jared. She told me that herself. No doubt you must have impressed her at the charity shoot."

McClure nodded and his phone buzzed. He held up his hand to the group in a *hold-on-a-minute* gesture and stood up and took the call in a corner of the room.

"Where?" McClure asked out loud.

"How long ago?" He asked into the phone.

"Okay," he said. "Alert all available units. Drury and I are rolling to the scene. Put the shopping center on lockdown."

"Our interview with Julia Dolenz will have to be postponed until perhaps tomorrow morning, Ron. Fred? We have an active shooter at a shopping center in Newport News. Let's roll."

"Yes sir," Drury barked.

"Marty? I'll call you when this is all wrapped up. Excuse us, gentlemen. Good work, Ron and Pete," McClure said, and with that, the two picked up their campaign hats and exited the conference room at a quickstep.

"Jared didn't get the time to tell you, Ron, that we may have caught a break on a possible suspect in this case as well as the other three that we're investigating," Tate said.

"Oh?" Chief Kelso said.

"Just this morning we got a tip from a witness that led us to a photograph of a man who could very well turn out to be the guy on the video surveillance footage that you just showed to us." Tate said as he pointed up at the blank screen.

"Does the guy have a name?" Kelso asked.

"You'll both be glad that you're sitting down," Tate said as he looked at the chief and Officer Langdon.

"The name on his website is Richard Dolenz."

"Jesus!" Kelso and Langdon blurted out simultaneously.

"Yep," Smith said. "And his photography business is listed with a Richmond address. We're very anxious to show his photograph to Julia Dolenz just as soon as Jared and his men close down this active shooting in Newport News."

"I'd say so," Kelso said. "Tell you what… We all know how these active shootings can play out. This could take us into tomorrow morning. Agreed?"

"Agreed," Tate said. "And I don't want to interview Ms. Dolenz without Jared being present. It sounds as if she might be comfortable and more forthcoming if he's there."

"So how about I give her a call today asking her to be available tomorrow morning?" Kelso said.

Marty looked at Kenny and they both nodded.

"Sounds good. We'll get rooms in town, and I'll get the chance to enjoy another dinner with my son, Robert, who is attending William and Mary," Tate said.

"That would be my Alma Mater," Pete Langdon said. "It's a great school. You must be proud of him."

"I am," Tate said. He looked back at Smith.

"Kenny, why don't you join Robert and me at dinner? He'd be thrilled to see you outside of the office."

"Are you buying?" Smith said with a grin on his face.

"Yes. Shit… Why not? Lizbeth and I are spoiling the boy as it is," Tate said with a smile.

He looked back at Ron Kelso.

"Jared told me about the charity shooting match, Ron," Tate said. "He told me that you were there too. Just out of curiosity… how good a shot is Julia Dolenz?"

154

"I'll let Jared confirm that, but, from what I saw that day, I'd say that Julia Dolenz could shoot the nuts off of a skunk from twenty-five feet away," Kelso said.

"She's one of the best shooters that I've seen - male or female - in Northern Virginia. She went head to head with Jared in the final combat round. He won, but, as Jared must have told you, she shot an impressive second place."

"She's better than me," Langdon said as he shook his head slightly.

"No shit?" Smith said.

"No shit," Langdon said. "And she prefers to shoot with a nine."

"A lot heavier than a .22 for a target match," Tate said.

Landon nodded again.

"So," Langdon began. "What do you suppose are the odds that this character named Richard Dolenz turns out to be a relation of Julia Dolenz? Like, maybe, even her son?"

"*That* would be a darlin' thing," Tate said, as he pointed his right hand across the table and 'shot' Langdon with his thumb and forefinger.

"I know all of us have other matters to attend to," Kelso said as he stood up. "So I'll make that call to Ms. Dolenz and we'll wait to hear back from Jared."

The others stood up as well, and shook hands and went in their different directions. Marty Tate, together with Kenny Smith, then drove the short distance to the Williamsburg Lodge and checked-in and he called his son from his room about another dinner get-together. His son was thrilled. After concluding the call, he felt a twinge of guilt about not being with Jared McClure and the other good guys in Newport News.

"Keep watch over everybody, won't you Lord?" he said as he unpacked his just-in-case overnight bag before he returned some calls back to his office in Manteo.

Chapter 27

The next morning, Lt. Jared McClure was at the Williamsburg Police Department to meet Marty Tate and drive over to the home of Ms. Julia Dolenz. Kenny Smith returned to Manteo at Tate's instruction. It was the start of the second day following the murder of Reginald White. The active shooting situation the night before in Newport News had been resolved peacefully, with the shooter surrendering himself to the authorities after firing several rounds of his semiautomatic into pieces of merchandise in a department store and demanding to speak to his former boss who had fired him the day before.

Tate met McClure and they rode together in his car the few blocks away to a fashionable street lined with impressive brick houses that mimicked the architecture of the colonial time period. The morning air was comfortable, but the weather people on the radio were calling for a typical hot day all up and down the peninsula with both the temperature as well as the dew point in the 90's.

"So," Tate said while sitting in the passenger seat. "How would you like to handle this?"

"I'll take the lead since she sort of knows me already," McClure said. "I'm still a little puzzled as to why she's called me into this case. The local P.D., though they are small, are quite competent enough to lead an investigation like this," he said as he turned the car into the driveway of the Dolenz residence.

"Chief Kelso told me yesterday that they've asked her if Reginald White had any enemies that would wish him injury or harm," Tate said.

"Yeah? What did she tell them?"

"That since Reginald was a divorce attorney, of course she imagined that his death could have been at the hands of a deranged party in one of the more nasty divorces that he had handled. She kept saying that she was confused about why anyone would remove his wedding ring finger. The local cops, of course, knew nothing about the other two murder victims and mutilations until after they had interviewed her and had checked the ViCap database."

"We'll have to clue her in on that as a way of introducing your involvement, I suppose," McClure said.

"Yes. And then there's the identity of this Richard Dolenz that we'll have to raise after we show her the picture that we got off of the website."

"If it is a relative of hers, I wonder what she or Reginald could have done to make this individual murderous." McClure said.

They both looked out the windshield at the house and its grounds. The lawn was cut and perfectly edged. The brick on the house appeared as if it had been recently power washed. Geraniums grew in splendor out of two large matching urns that adorned both sides of the wooden main door which had a polished brass knocker as its centerpiece just below a small lookout window. The hedges and boxwoods were as neatly trimmed as they were in the Historic Area of town. In a few words, the place quietly screamed out *money*, *prestige*, and *influence*. It could easily be a cover picture for *Home & Garden* magazine.

"Nice pad," Tate said.

"Yeah. Not too shabby," McClure said. "Shall we?"

"We shall," Tate said as they both exited the vehicle and walked up the stone steps to the front door and knocked.

Expecting a costumed servant to answer the door, both gentlemen were surprised to be greeted by Julia herself. She looked as Jared remembered her, except for the slight bags around her eyes - no doubt caused by grief and crying. To Marty she appeared petite and trim with an athletic build. He couldn't fathom that the woman before him was a crack shot with a 9mm pistol. She had brown, shoulder - length hair that she wore loosely. She had on a powder-blue, short sleeved, form-fitting cotton top; blue jeans, and fashionable casual shoes. She held out her hand to McClure who shook it.

"Hello Lt. McClure," she said. "So good of you to come. When I last saw you at the charity event in Newport News, you had given me your business card with an offer of help if I ever needed it. Do you remember?"

"Of course. And please call me Jared."

"Indeed. And I daresay that I need help now more than at any other time that I care to remember. And who's your companion?"

Julia extended her hand out to Marty Tate and he shook it with his large right hand that seemed to swallow hers up.

"Marty Tate, ma'am. I'm the sheriff of Dare County in North Carolina's Outer Banks. Jared and I will explain further."

"Ah," she said. "Then, by all means come in. I can use all the help that I can get with this nasty business."

The inside of the home was as neat and tidy as the outside with vases of fresh cut flowers set down in every room. The stone entryway gleamed. The hardwood floors adjoining were a rich, dark brown with accent rugs of different dimensions and designs strategically placed about. There stood a tall, cherry wood high boy with glass doors in the living room where she led them. She offered them to take seats wherever they pleased.

"Cordelia?" She called out.

"Yes, Julia?" A soft voice replied from the next room.

"Please confirm my appointment at the funeral home for later this afternoon."

"Of course, Julia," the soft voice confirmed.

"Cordelia is my electronic personal assistant," she explained to the two men. "I find her to be indispensable to me during this saddest of times."

She took a seat opposite them in a red Queen Anne chair with a back that extended higher than her head.

The interview began with McClure asking her to repeat and recall everything that she had already told the Williamsburg police, explaining to her that this might jump-start a detail that she may have forgotten or overlooked. She complied, and her recollections matched up entirely with what she had told the local police. Tate jumped into the conversation as delicately as he could put it.

"Ms. Dolenz," he began.

"Please call me Julia. You're here trying to help me, and I appreciate that."

"Yes, ma'am. I mean, yes, Julia. The reason that I am here with Jared is that he and I are working to solve two other homicides, as well as an attempted third, that have all the bearings of Mr. White's murder." Tate explained. He continued.

"One was committed last year in Virginia. A student at the University of Virginia that went missing one year ago, whose body was found by law enforcement this June. Another murder took place

158

this past late June within my jurisdiction on the Outer Banks. And a few weeks ago, a victim survived a murderous attack at the hands of who we believe to be the same person. A male suspect. This attempted murder also took place on the Outer Banks."

"I see. When you say, 'all the bearings,' are you referring to the missing wedding ring finger?" She held up her left hand.

"Yes, ma'am. I mean, yes, Julia. The two other murder victims were male and their wedding ring fingers were also missing. It's what we in law enforcement refer to as the killer's signature," Tate said.

"Oh my heavens," she said as she drew her right hand up to her chin.

"Do you have any living relatives here in the states?" McClure asked with the foreknowledge that she had emigrated from Great Britain.

"Yes. One son. An only child. His name is Richard," she said.

Tate and McClure traded controlled looks before Tate eased out the next question.

"Does he live quite far from here?"

"Oh, no," she said. "He lives just an hour away in Richmond in one of those awfully high - priced warehouse apartments near the James River."

"I see," Tate said, as he looked over and tossed the proverbial interrogation baton back into McClure's lap.

"Is Richard aware that Mr. White is deceased?" McClure asked.

"Yes," she said. "I telephoned him yesterday and told him. He said that he was dreadfully sorry about my loss. It was a very brief call."

"Has your son, Richard, ever been in trouble with the law?" McClure asked.

"As far as I know, he's never been arrested," she said as she crossed her legs right over left and placed her hands on her knee.

She studied her petite hands. Her mind raced. She looked up and past the two men to the bay window. She was as still as a statue.

Well, that's not to say that when Richard was in 8th grade a local boy fell under a truck whilst he was riding his bike. The police came 'round asking all the parents of the classmates about it, as they

159

had found the doomed child's bike had been tampered with so that the front wheel would fall off... Would they please know anything about that?

Then there was Richard's high school classmate at Christchurch School who perished behind the wheel of his car that had plunged headlong into the back of a semi-trailer truck. Once again, the police came 'round after their crime scene investigators had determined that the brake lines of the boy's car had been cut, and would she know anything about that? And last year, a college student went missing from the University of Virginia, where Richard was studying. And now he's been found dead. And his wedding ring finger was found to be missing...

"Julia?" McClure said aloud as he perceived her thousand-yard stare off into the distance as she stroked her chin with her right hand.

"I'm sorry," she said as her gaze returned to the room and the two men in front of her. She uncrossed her legs and sat straighter in the chair.

"Oh, how awfully rude of me," she said. "Would either of you care for something to drink? Coffee? Iced tea? Water?"

Both men shook their heads. McClure continued.

"Did Richard know Mr. White?" He asked.

"No," she said. "Richard knew who Reginald *was* and that we were getting married. I showed Richard's picture to Reginald, but the two never had the chance to meet face to face."

Tate pulled out the picture he had tucked into his tunic and unfolded the paper.

"Does this man resemble your son, Richard?" he asked as he slipped the photo across the room in her direction.

She took it into her small hands and studied it. Unable to speak for the moment, she nodded her head in ascent.

"Is that Richard?" McClure asked as he pointed at the photo. Another nod.

"Forgive my intrusion, Julia. But would Richard have *any* possible reason to wish Reginald injury or harm?" Tate asked.

She shook her head as she looked at the photo.

Christ! My suspicions are now confirmed. I can think of five thousand reasons a month that you'd want Reginald dead, you fucking little rotter! You murderous son of mine! Five thousand

160

*fucking dollars a month held back, and that's what Reggie died for?
Thirty-five hundred quid?! If you've done this to Reggie, I swear I
will hunt you down and kill you myself. You don't deserve to be fed
three squares a day in some prison and watch the telly until you're
old and gray. The police are questioning me about you! Again! You
must have done this to Reggie, you bloody, miserable piece of shit...*

She composed herself and handed the photo back to Tate.

"Where did you find this photograph?" She asked.

"It came from a website that advertises wedding
photography, if that makes any sense," Tate said.

"It does," she said. "As far as I know, that would be his
occupation."

She leaned over towards them in her chair.

"I'll ask you both plainly. Do you suspect him for these
crimes, gentlemen?"

There it was. The question cut across the air and space and
dangled there until it was dashed away by McClure.

"I'm afraid so, Julia," he said. "There was a witness to the
attempted murder on the Outer Banks that Marty had mentioned. She
came across this photo on the internet and came forward. This was
before we knew that Mr. White had been murdered. The photo
matches a police sketch that was drawn up after the first homicide in
June on the Outer Banks. And, when I say 'match,' there's no doubt
that it's the same man. I'm sorry."

She looked down at the area rug under her feet and held out
her hands as if she were praying. But she wasn't. She shook her head
back and forth slowly.

"I'm sorry to pry, but this is a homicide investigation," Tate
said. "We are forced to ask questions that may sound insensitive or
even intrusive."

"I quite understand," Julia said. "What is it?"

"Was Richard receiving any financial assistance from either
you or Mr. White?"

"Why do ask?"

"You mentioned a moment ago that Richard lives in an
expensive apartment. Your home here in Williamsburg is handsome
and opulent. Mr. White made a great deal of money, we're told.
Photographer's like Richard *don't* make a lot of money..." He
spread his hands.

161

She sat back in her chair and put her arms around herself.

"Yes. I see where you're going... quite right... quite right."

Her eyes looked up and pointed left. McClure and Tate patiently waited. In essence, Tate, in his latest question, had telegraphed to Julia that he didn't believe her response to the earlier question about Richard having no cause to mean injury or harm to Reginald. He was a southern gentleman. He wasn't calling her a liar out loud. He was giving her another chance to be forthright. To Tate, most mothers almost always knew their children better that what they let on in public. She cleared her throat.

"Right after college," she began.

"Excuse me, Julia," McClure said. "Which college?"

She looked over at him directly. Her eyes met his.

"He graduated from the University of Virginia." She said.

"I see." McClure said. "Please continue?"

"Right after college, I began to supplement his small income with a monthly allowance." She paused to see if they wanted to hear more details before she continued.

"What was the amount per month?" Tate asked.

"Thirty-five hundred quid," she said.

"That's five-thousand dollars a month. That should have made him quite comfortable, indeed," McClure said.

"And when did you - or Mr. White - cut him off?" Tate said, in a matter-of-fact way.

"More than a month ago, Sheriff Tate. After Reggie and I announced our engagement. It was actually Reggie's idea. We were gradually reducing his allowance in half until he would be forced to live independently of the monthly stipend. We were going to put the money in a trust for Richard instead. We told him as much. I can see that you're highly experienced and that you're nobody's fool, Sheriff Tate. My compliments to you." She said.

"I confess that I can't take all the credit, Julia. Jared and I spoke with an FBI psychological investigator about our possible offender," Tate said.

"One of those profiler people I see in some of the crime shows on the telly?" She said.

"Yes."

"Extraordinary," she said. "Do go on. What did he or she have to say?"

"That whoever was committing these crimes was being both spoiled and denied. Things were being withheld, including affection. Rejection was a word that he used several times when he talked to us. Lastly, he said that this person was raging against a strong authority figure."

"Such as his mother," Julia said as she once more cast her eyes up and to her left as she jostled slightly in her chair.

"Such as his mother," Tate said. "Hence my question about money being cut off. That could have been the trigger in the case of Mr. White, but, something else and much more dated in time would have to be the explanation for the other previous murders."

She looked back at Tate directly.

"Are you implying that I may have damaged Richard psychologically somehow when he was growing up? You must understand that I tried to do the very best by him as a single mother." She wiped a tear from her eye.

Tate held out both his large arms and hands as if he were trying to stop a skidding truck that was heading towards him.

"No ma'am. I didn't mean to imply anything." He lowered his arms, paused, and then spoke again.

"'Those who live only to satisfy their *own* sinful nature will harvest decay and death from that sinful nature,'" he said. "Richard is responsible for his behavior."

"Galatians 6:8." She said softly. "Once again, I'm impressed, Sheriff Tate. It's a line I used to share with Richard. Apparently, I've failed as a mother awfully." Another tear began to well-up in her eye.

"I'm sorry again, for your loss," Tate said. "And Jared and I are both sorry to have to be the ones to tell you that we think that your son was involved in all of this - for his own selfish motives. Whatever they are."

"Did Richard know that it was Mr. White's idea to withhold the allowance?" McClure asked.

She nodded as she took out a tissue from her pocket and wiped her eyes.

"I told him weeks ago by telephone," she said.

163

"We need to find him and talk with him, and soon." McClure said.

She nodded and got up from her chair. She walked into the kitchen as the two men waited. They both stood up. She returned with a small slip of paper that she handed to McClure.

"I've recorded his phone number and address here. How soon will you be going to see him?"

"We'll be heading to Richmond presently," McClure said. "We have a search warrant for his residence."

Once again she nodded, then together they walked to the front door.

"One additional thing, Julia," McClure said.

"Of course," she said.

"We'd appreciate it if you didn't call him to tell him that we're on our way to take him into custody for questioning," He said.

"You have my word," she said. "If he's responsible for Reggie's death, as you both believe that he is and of course for the deaths of the others, then Richard will not receive any assistance from me. He will have to answer and atone for this on his own."

Tate and McClure nodded. They were making their way out the door when she spoke again.

"And gentlemen? If he's guilty… I want him prosecuted to the very fullest extent of the law. Do you have my meaning?"

"The death penalty for homicide in the first degree is still in force in both Virginia and North Carolina," Tate said.

"Good," she said. "So as it should be, in brutal and senseless cases such as this."

She closed the door and went back inside.

The men returned to their car. McClure started the engine.

"I wouldn't want to piss her off unnecessarily," Tate said.

"Especially, if she were armed," McClure said as he put the car in reverse, backed out the driveway, and headed for the interstate and to Richmond.

* * * * *

"Well," Julia said as she watched the policemen drive away. "That settles it."

She walked briskly to her kitchen and retrieved her mobile phone and punched in a number.

At his flat in Richmond, Richard's phone rang and buzzed.

"Hello?" He said as he picked it up.

"Richard," Julia said. "It's me. I'm calling to say that I've been thinking things over since Reggie's death and reconsidering the possibility that I may have been too willing to agree with him about your allowance."

"You don't say," Richard said, keeping the tone of his voice as neutral as he could.

"Yes," she said. "I've come to realize that you're my only flesh and blood, and as such we need to talk about your allowance as well as the future. We need to have a face to face discussion. How soon could you come 'round to see me?"

Terry was right! Richard thought to himself. *Things are looking brighter just as he said they would!*

"I could leave straight away," he said. "I can be there in an hour, if you'd like."

"Yes. I believe that would work as I have other commitments in the afternoon. See you shortly then."

"Indeed," he said before he rang off.

Richard hiked his arms up high in the air and danced a jig around his kitchen. After he gathered a few items from his bedroom he left his flat, got in his car, and sped off to the southeast bound for Williamsburg.

165

Chapter 28

The traffic was typically busy along I - 64 Westbound as
Jared McClure and Marty Tate debriefed their interview with Julia
Dolenz and planned their next steps on their way to Richmond. First,
McClure placed a call to Fred Drury.

"Fred? It's Jared. Marty and I have just left the Dolenz
residence in Billsburg. I've got a phone number. I'd like you to pull
the LUD's on it after you get a judge to grant a court order for the
phone company. Are you ready? Here's the number."

He gave it to him. McClure was referring to "local usage
details," which is a list of a person's incoming and outgoing phone
calls over a specified period of time. He continued.

"When you're finished with that, let's get busy with a
Stingray phone tracker and see if we can get lucky and detect the
movements of this guy Dolenz in real time. Also, send two units,
silent on approach, and have them wait about a half a mile away
from the following address in Richmond. Also, tell them to be on the
lookout for any white BMW sedans they might see in the vicinity. If
they do, have them call in."

He gave Drury the address that Julia Dolenz had provided.

"When we're just a few minutes out, I'll notify them and our
three units can proceed to the apartment address. If we're in luck,
we'll be able to take Mr. Dolenz into custody and return with him to
Williamsburg for questioning. Copy that?"

"Copy that," Drury said, and he disconnected the call.

"What's your take on the relationship between Julia Dolenz
and her son?" McClure said.

"I'd say it's a strained one," Tate said. "It took two questions
before she came clean about the outrageously large monthly
allowance that she was sending him. And she didn't volunteer that it
was Reginald White's idea to suspend it until you asked her directly.
And when she said that she didn't think that Richard had ever been
arrested, it hinted that he may had some run-ins with the police when
he was younger. It was a carefully worded answer."

"I agree. Maybe the allowance was really just payment to
keep Richard out of her life. Her reaction about the death penalty

was damned cold, even if Richard did kill her Reginald. It makes me think that she suspects him of his murder like we do." McClure said.

"Most mothers know their kids better than they think they do," Tate said.

"Yep," McClure said before he pinned the accelerator and passed an eighteen wheeler that was driving at the posted speed limit.

Chapter 29

Back in Williamsburg, Richard Dolenz pulled up into his mother's driveway in his white BMW 5 Series. He reached across the center console over to the passenger seat and picked up a fancy bouquet of funereal flowers that had set him back nearly one hundred dollars at a florist on North Boundary Street. He had attached a note inside a small envelope that was taped to the clear cellophane that wrapped around the large spray of lilies and gladioli and greenery. It was the pre-printed kind that all florists sell. There were no personal remarks on the small card. It simply read "With Deepest Sympathy," and he had scrawled his signature to it. Truthfully, it may as well have read, "Eat Shit and Die," and he would have signed that, too. Still, it was the disingenuous thought that counted, he figured to himself as he got out of the car. He was wearing a long-sleeved powder blue shirt and a cream colored linen jacket over jeans and tennis shoes. He placed the flowers on top of the warm hood of the car as he made an adjustment under the jacket near the small of his back before he once more picked up the bouquet and walked up to the front door and rang the bell.

From inside, it sounded like the same elegant bell sound that he remembered when he was raised as a boy here. That is, during the times when he wasn't being parked by his mum at friends' houses or engaging in activities after school that she forced him to join, or sending him off to schools that he didn't want to attend. He wanted to pursue his studies at the nearby College of William and Mary. But no. That would never do for Julia. If he wanted his college studies as well as room and board completely paid for, she said he'd have to go away to the University of Virginia.

Even during those years not long passed he remembered staying at university during breaks because his mother always seemed to have trips abroad planned during the same time period. He felt like fucking Ebenezer Scrooge lolling about campus while his friends were enjoying holidays such as Christmas back at home. Julia never trusted him with keys to the house in Williamsburg, and the bitch had even taken the liberty of having all the locks changed when he was in his junior year. Still, she sent money if he had cared

168

to travel, and during one summer break he discovered the Outer Banks and learned that it was a popular place for weddings.

Upon spying at him through the door, Julia returned to the living room and to the tall, cherry wood highboy. She pulled out a drawer at waist level and took out her Glock 19 9mm pistol. As she was properly trained to do, she drove the gun mechanism forward with her right hand as she held the slide bar with her left and jacked a round up into the chamber of the gun. She made sure that the safety was in the "off" position, then she returned the weapon to the drawer. Before she walked back to the front entranceway, she called out to the adjoining living room.

"Cordelia... Please contact the funeral home and re - schedule my afternoon appointment for 6pm this evening."

"Of course, Julia," the machine said by way of response.

She unlatched the door and opened it.

"Hello mum," Richard said as he held out the bouquet of flowers.

She took the bouquet and smelled the lilies.

"Richard. These are quite lovely. Please come in."

She turned her back on him and walked away towards the kitchen. He closed the front door and followed her. Once inside the kitchen, she opened a cabinet and reached for a tall, crystal vase and placed the flowers inside. She opened another cabinet and removed a tall glass as well as a small glass vial that she placed in the corner of the cabinet the day before. Keeping the vial and the glass out of view she walked over to the refrigerator, opened the door and returned to a nearby counter and poured out a glass of iced tea. She closed the refrigerator door and turned around and walked back towards Richard, holding out the glass. He accepted it, and took a good swig of the tea. It was his favorite flavor, mango.

"You'll have to drink that up quickly and be on your way," she said as she took a pull on her glass of ice water. "I have several important appointments today, including one this afternoon."

He studied her for a bit before he polished off his iced tea and set the glass on the counter next to the sink.

"I was invited here, remember? Once again, I'm sorry for your loss," he said.

"I didn't ask for your sympathy, Richard. And I did summon you here." She said as she walked over to his empty glass, rinsed it under the sink and set it on the drying rack. She turned around to look back at him, but he had disappeared. She heard the closing of the bathroom door that was down the hallway. She followed him and stood outside the door where she could plainly hear him retching. She returned to the kitchen.

When he re - appeared, his skin appeared clammy.

"Sorry for rushing off like that, but the bloody fast food that I had to eat disagreed with me terribly. As I was saying and I'll say it again, I'm sorry for your loss."

She rolled her eyes.

"Whoever murdered Reggie cut off his wedding ring finger. Did you know that? Can you imagine how that's affected me?" She said.

"My God," he said. "That's disgusting. What a ghoulish thing to do."

She noted that he didn't ask if the amputation was done when Reggie was alive.

"I discovered his body as I told you on the phone, but I didn't mention the mutilation. I keep wondering if the killer was hoping that I'd see that."

"What an awful thought. How dreadful. I'm so sorry."

"Richard, if you were truly sympathetic to my situation, you wouldn't have…"

"Wouldn't have *what?*" He said.

"I meant to say, that if you were truly sympathetic to my situation you would have come 'round when Reggie was alive. To meet him and get to know him. To comprehend what a great man that he was and to celebrate our happiness." She crossed her arms.

"Like I told you over the phone, I don't have a lot of extra money lying about," he said.

"You could have taken that 70 quid you probably spent on flowers and put petrol into that fancy car of yours and drove down to meet Reggie. Enough said. Look, I'd really prefer that you leave this minute," she said as she pointed towards the front entranceway.

"No," he said. "Not until we've settled my allowance dispute."

He walked quickly past her to the front living area of the house and sat in one of his favorite chairs located in front of a large bay window.

170

Julia looked at her watch and entered the room and stood by the tall highboy.

"So, you think that with Reggie out of the way, that I've changed my mind completely about your allowance? Is that what you thought?"

"Something like that, I suppose. After all, doesn't your only son - your own flesh and blood - who's still alive and well mean more to you than a dead fiancé?"

She placed her arms behind her back in a casual posture and maneuvered herself so that she could easily open the drawer which held her pistol if need be.

"Truthfully? No. No, his beloved memory - as well as his wishes - mean more to me than you ever will, considering the present circumstances. So, as I said, I have arrangements to make. Leave this instant, please. We have nothing more to talk about." She jerked her head towards the door.

Richard put his right hand behind his back and stood up.

"You're using that bloody fucking 'no' word again!" He roared. "Who the *fuck* do you think you're talking to, *bitch*!?"

From behind his back he brought out the .22 Browning Buckmaster complete with the menacing silencer and pointed at her.

"Well, well, well," she said calmly. "I can see that Richard has left the room and his friend Terry Grant has taken his place. Is *that* it?"

He nodded his head vigorously. He was beginning to perspire around his temples.

"I won't grant an audience to a madman brandishing a pop gun and pointing it at me. Take a seat *Terry*, and put the pistol on the table next to you if you'd like. Then, we'll talk a bit."

"You promise? You're not joking?" He said with a tincture of astonishment in his voice.

"No, Terry. Mumsie isn't joking. Lower the weapon and have a seat." She gestured with her left arm.

Without moving his eyes away from her, he took a seat back in his chair and placed the pistol on the small table next to him. He took in a shallow breath of air and allowed both his arms to extend over the armrests as he used to do as a boy.

"You were nearly six when Richard and I created you. Remember?" Julia said. "We had left England when you were three.

When we settled here and on various occasions when I watched you playing with your toys, I took pity on the fact that you were an only child. I mean, knowing that I didn't *want* any more children after I had *you*. So, I decided that you needed a friend who could accompany you on all of your imaginary adventures. A friend that I wouldn't have to take care of. A dependable, imaginary friend who I named, 'Terry.' Do you recall?"

He nodded his head but said nothing. His eyes seemed to be fixating at the floor. He rubbed his temple with his right hand, then he rubbed both his hands against his pant knees. His skin felt increasingly clammy.

"So," she continued. "I came up with the first name of 'Terry,' and Richard came up with the last name of 'Grant.' He told me that he often enjoyed watching the old Cary Grant movies on the telly with me, and would it be alright if Terry could have the last name 'Grant.'"

"Yes," he said still staring at the floor.

"It was all such innocent fun for years, but then I'd uncover dead cats buried in the flower bed in the backyard near the potting shed. I asked you if you knew how they had gotten there, and you told me that Terry had placed them there, because they had scratched Richard and had hissed at him and bit him. That gave me quite a turn. That was about the time that I was getting concerned that the imaginary game was going adrift into dangerous territory.
Then, when you were in eighth grade, a young boy was killed here in town whilst he was out riding on his bike..."

"Sean O'Casey," he said without expression.

"Yes. Yes, that's the name the policeman gave to me when they came round conducting their inquiries. I protected you from any suspicion because that's what good mothers do, of course. But then, four years later, a boy from your boarding school was killed while driving his car."

"Clive McDonald. High five for Clive. He's no longer alive...," he said, again without expression. He coughed.

"Yes. You sound glad for it. And just this year, most recently I daresay, the police uncovered the body of a young man who had been attending your college."

"Kevin Berkley," he said.

"Was that his name?"

172

"Yes. Poof. No more Kevin. Kevin hasn't phoned home..." He said as if he were in a trance and talking to himself.

"I think that you should shut up, Terry, and let Richard talk to me. It's about his money that we'll be talking about." She said.

"No!" He said. He relished the opportunity to use that word against her for a change. "I'm Richard's fixer. You have to settle things with me."

"I see. Well, the police told me - just this morning actually - that the young man's wedding ring finger had been cut off," she said.

"They called you this morning?"

"Actually, they came 'round here in the flesh making inquiries regarding Reginald's death."

He looked up at her momentarily. He was still perspiring in the air conditioned space. His breathing became more rapid.

"Did Terry Grant kill this poor Kevin fellow?" She said.

He nodded.

"And what did Kevin ever do to deserve being killed and mutilated?"

"He stole Richard's girl." He said without emotion.

"Why was his wedding ring finger amputated?"

"He wasn't going to need it anymore," he said. "I wasn't going to permit them to get married."

"How many others has Terry killed in the past year?" she demanded.

"Two."

"And one of them was my poor Reggie?"

He looked up at her. His eyeballs were like laser lights burning into hers. But they were as lifeless as a play doll's. He nodded.

"Enough with the excessive chit-chat. You've said nothing about my money. I want my money. I want what's coming to me. Father would wish it that way."

She cocked her head back up towards the ceiling and cackled an ugly laugh of sorts.

"Your father?! George?" She straightened her head and looked back at him.

"Quite right. Quite right," she said. "Let's discuss your father shall we? And then I'll be sure to dole out what's coming to you."

"Splendid," he said, as he made a rolling, *let's-get- on-with-it* gesture with his left hand. He coughed again.

"As I've told you many times, your father was a practicing physician in the village where we lived. That's where he had his clinic and saw his patients. He had a heart condition for which he was prescribed digitalis, which seemed to keep him right as rain."

Richard made the rolling gesture again.

"So, one evening at dinner, your father told me that he was in love with a younger woman. One of his patients, actually. It was a complete shock to me. Anyway, he said that he intended to seek a divorce and to provide for you and me with a modest monthly stipend. He, of course, would move out and find a flat, but he would keep the clinic as well as the lion's share of wealth that was created through his income."

"Why haven't you told me this before?" Richard said sounding a bit out of breath.

"Because I didn't want you to know that murder was running through your veins." She said.

"What's this?" He said, sounding absolutely puzzled.

"I wasn't going to permit George to run off with his young trollop and take away the lifestyle to which I had become accustomed. So, I carried out a plan. I studied the internet, which was not as sophisticated as it is today, but I found what I was looking for. I went to George's beloved greenhouse one day, put on some gloves, and took some cuttings from his prized monkshood. You see, even the slight contact with the flowers can cause the fingers of one's hands to become numb. I then made a tincture with the cuttings and mixed it into his hand cream that he was so fond of. Anyway, two mornings later, I served him his breakfast as usual and went back into the kitchen for something, and when I came back to the dining room, I found him with his head down inside his bowl of bubble and squeak. I could see quite plainly that the cheating lout was dead. As dead as a doornail. So, I turned on my crocodile tears and called the police crying to them to come 'round quick as my husband must have had a massive heart attack."

"That's how he died? A heart attack? Is that what you're telling me?" He said in a raspy voice.

"No!" She said. "Stop being so thick in the head! I'm telling you that I *murdered* your father, George. With poison that I had

174

concocted from his flower bed. How deliciously and deviously ironic it was. I did him in with something like this," she said as she took her right arm out from behind her back, dipped her hand into her pocket and removed a small glass vial.

"What is that?" He said as he pulled at his shirt around his neck with his right hand.

"It's called aconite. It's a very strong poison. Only one gram does the job completely. It paralyzes the respiratory system, you see. And it's very hard to detect during the course of a normal autopsy."

"No!" He cried out. "I can't believe this!"

"You'd better believe this, you ungrateful snot! I had to suffer through a very nasty inquest back then. Naturally, I cast suspicion on your father's new girlfriend and the police dragged her through the bloody weeds. But, in the end, they couldn't prove that either one of us had killed George. His ancient heart condition, you see? So, I got away with murder and I had claim to all his money."

"No!" He cried out again as he put his hands over his ears.

"So, all the money that you have been receiving has come from me at my very own discretion. Your father had no choice in it. And now I find that you repay my generosity by killing Reginald? And you've come here threatening me with that pop gun of yours? I'll bet that it's the same one you used to shoot my poor defenseless Reggie."

She turned and reached her hand into the drawer of the highboy and grabbed her pistol and turned around quickly and pointed it at her son who was now leaning back in his chair, his right hand over his chest, and held out his left as if to block a bullet.

"I executed your father for his crime of lust, and now I'm going to execute you for murdering my Reggie and for all the others you've maimed. I'm not going to permit you to drag my good name through the mud the way your cheating father did."

She held up the vial again in her left hand.

"You see, I whipped up this little batch of aconite yesterday. You do know that I grow monkshood in my flower garden out back, don't you, Terry?"

He talked to her in a raspy voice.

"You wouldn't kill… your own son," he gasped.

"No. I won't have to. The *aconite* will though." She continued to hold up the small glass vial in her left hand and shook it. "Your iced tea. Remember, *Terry?*"

He shook his head back and forth and turned convulsing in his chair to his right before he reached for his weapon and clutched it to his chest. He made a croaking sound, and fell over on to the floor.

"You see, Terry, you think you're Richard's fixer, but what you've actually done is fixed him permanently, and yourself too. Cheerio, I won't be seeing either of you again."

She put the vial away, lowered her weapon and approached him and kneeled beside him. All was quiet. She placed her left hand on his throat. She felt no pulse. She knew that he was dead. She had laced the iced tea with enough poison to kill two grown men.

She felt a certain satisfactory scorn as she stood up and moved down the hallway to the linen closet, removed an old pillowcase, and returned to the kitchen. She placed Richard's used glass, as well as the almost empty vial which held the aconite, inside the pillowcase then took a heavy meat tenderizer from one of the drawers and smashed the glass into small bits.

She took the pillowcase and opened up the door of the kitchen that led to the backyard. It made its usual loud squeak as she walked back to her potting shed. She opened the wooden door and selected a planting shovel. She heard the loud metallic chipping sound of cardinal song as she looked around the quiet yard. Nothing was stirring with the exception of a couple of squirrels chasing each other around a tree. She selected a flower bed on the side of the shed where she dug a hole of approximately three feet in depth, deposited the pillowcase and its contents, and covered the hole with a couple of red geranium plants, and returned to the house. The door squeaked again as she entered the kitchen. It was time to turn on her crocodile tears, find her phone, and call the police to tell them a story that she had made up in order to notify and explain the demise of her son, Richard.

She walked to the edge of the kitchen and stared out at Richard's lifeless body.

"It's as they say here in the States, Richard, payback's a bitch. And so the bloody hell am I," she said out loud before she punched the speed dial button on her phone for 911.

In no more than ten minutes time, a swarm of police and first responder vehicles light bars flashing, were parked in front of her house and Chief Ron Kelso and Officer Pete Langdon were in the lead car.

Chapter 30

The scene inside the home of Julia Dolenz was one of controlled professional mayhem as medical technicians were busy examining the body of Richard Dolenz, still balled up in its catatonic state of death on the living room floor. Crime scene unit technicians were snapping pictures, others were taking fiber samples. Meanwhile, Chief Kelso and Officer Pete Langdon were questioning a seemingly shaken Julia in her kitchen. She sat in a chair at the table, a handkerchief out which she used to blot her eyes which occasionally would flood with tears of rage, not sadness. Both Kelso and Langdon stood and noticed that her attire was pristine with the exception of some traces of mud and dirt on her shoes.

"I'm so sorry for your most recent loss, Ms. Dolenz. Please tell us what happened here this morning," Kelso said.

She shook her head back and forth, her shoulders were drooped. She started wringing the handkerchief in her petite hands.

"It's as I told your office on the 911 call," she began. "Richard came here and confronted me about getting back his allowance that Reginald and I had suspended. I had no idea that's what set him off so. He confessed to killing Reggie over it! Christ!"

"Do you know of anyone with the name of Terry Grant?" Langdon asked.

"Who?" She looked up at him.

"The white BMW parked out front in your driveway," Langdon said. "It's registered to a Terry Grant with a Richmond address."

"Oh. I see," she said. "That was Richard's alter ego. His imaginary friend from youth. He was quite insane. He had what they call a split personality. One personality, kind. The other, evil. I thought it was harmless when he was small, but then he grew up and continued "the game" as he called it and it made me uneasy. But I couldn't bring myself to commit my only child. Besides, I didn't think he was a danger to himself or others. So, I tried to distance myself. I sent him away to boarding school and later to college. But this morning he claimed that this Terry Grant character had killed a number of people over the years, and most recently my Reggie.

178

After he confessed to these crimes, he took out his weapon and pointed it at me and said that he would kill me if he didn't get his allowance back. He was totally 'round the bend and out of control as I've never seen him before. Raving! And then, quite unexpectedly, he had a seizure and collapsed on the floor as you've found him. It was awful! His father George died from a heart attack back in England years ago. He had congenital heart disease. Perhaps Richard inherited that. I've lost Reggie and my son in the span of a few short days. My god."

"Again, we're sorry that this happened," Kelso said. "Would you kindly show us where you were and where Richard was when he took out his weapon?"

She nodded and arose from her chair in the kitchen and strolled the few paces into the living room and stood in front of the tall highboy.

"I was standing here," she said. "Richard was sitting in that chair." She pointed to where her son's body lay.

"Quite suddenly, he stood up and took out a gun from behind his back. It must've been hidden by his jacket. Anyway, that's when he pointed the gun at me and before I knew it, he collapsed on to the floor where you see him now."

Kelso and Langdon exchanged looks.

"You're quite sure that he was standing when he took out his weapon?" Langdon said.

"Yes. Yes, of course," she said.

"Alright, we can all return to the kitchen then," Kelso said. When they returned to the kitchen Julia took her chair and Langdon asked the next question.

"Would you tell us the names of the people he claimed to have killed with this split personality of his?"

"He claimed to have started killing people when he was in the eighth grade," she said. Then she named the rest, as Richard had confessed, and Langdon wrote them down in his slim notepad. Kelso and he both recognized the name of Kevin Berkley.

"Would you please excuse me, ma'am?" Kelso said as he walked into an adjoining family room, took out his cell phone and dialed Jared McClure.

McClure picked up on the caller I.D. on his phone and answered it as he sent the call to the car's speakers so that Tate could hear. They were in downtown Richmond and heading to the address of Richard Dolenz.

"Hey Ron," McClure said. "What've you got?"

"A real shit storm, Jared. I'm at the home of Julia Dolenz. Her son, Richard is here too. Except that *he's* as dead as Ronald Reagan." Kelso said.

"What?!" McClure and Tate responded.

"You heard me right."

"How?" McClure said as he pinned the accelerator and fishtailed the car as he turned the vehicle around back towards I-64 East.

"The fuck if *I* know," Kelso said. "We haven't been here that long. He was armed with a .22. Julia Dolenz said that he threated to kill her before he croaked from a seizure. She said he suffered from a split personality. But, the location of the body at the crime scene doesn't seem to match her story. You best get back here a.s.a.p."

McClure hit the switch for the blue light bar and the other for the siren.

"Copy that," he said. "We're on our way. *Out.*" He disconnected the call.

Kelso returned to the kitchen. Officer Langdon jerked his head towards the living room.

"Excuse us again, ma'am?" Langdon said as he and Kelso walked back into the living room to talk to the EMT techs that were placing Richard Dolenz's remains inside a body bag and preparing for transport to the morgue.

"Heart attack?" Chief Kelso asked.

"Sure looks that way, Chief," a young blonde tech said as she was zipping up the body bag. "We'll know a lot more when…"

"When we get him on the table… I know. Thanks," Kelso said. "Let me ask you something else?"

"Sure," the tech said.

"Was this guy sitting in this chair when he suffered his seizure?"

"I'd say I'm positive that he was sitting here by the way the body is positioned. It looks as if he rolled to his right and fell off of a chair clutching the gun to his chest. His left shoulder would have made the first impact with the floor. I've seen this many times when called to a residence where an elderly person has died from a heart attack."

"So, he wasn't standing up when he suffered his seizure?" Langdon asked.

"No sir. If he had been standing, his body would be positioned quite differently, further away from the chair and laying with his upper body pointed towards the kitchen."

"Okay," Kelso said. "Thanks again."

"No problem," the tech said.

Kelso stood next to Langdon while they looked at the body of Richard Dolenz being carted away.

"Why in the hell would this guy be sitting in a chair when he threatened his mother with a gun?" Kelso said. "Julia Dolenz can't be telling the truth about what happened here."

"It doesn't add up to me, either. We'll run the ballistics to see if it's the same gun that killed Reginald White, of course. I wonder where she keeps her weapon."

"Let's make sure that we ask."

As they walked to another corner of the room. Langdon pointed towards an electronic device that resembled a small tower.

"What is that?" Kelso said.

"It's one of those new electronic administrative assistants. Google makes one. Amazon make one. This one's from a company named Timespan. The device is called Cordelia." Langdon explained.

"So? Why should we give a shit about it?" Kelso said.

"You see how that green strobe light keeps circling the base of the device?"

"Yeah."

"That means it's turned on. It's recording what's said here in this space."

"Really?" Kelso said.

"Really. It may have been on the whole time that her son was here. It may have recorded the entire altercation she's describing. If

181

that's the case, their conversation is sitting on a Timespan server someplace."

"No shit?" Kelso said.

"I shit you not, boss." Langdon said. "There was a story about a case that came out in Arkansas in 2016. A guy named Bates was charged with the 2015 murder of a man named Collins. Amazon got served a warrant to request the audio files from Bates' device. Amazon griped about consumers' privacy rights, but eventually, they conceded and turned over what they had. I think we should do the same in this case and see what we can shake out of Timespan."

"I like your thinking, Pete," Kelso said. "Get a judge today and tell them that this is urgent."

"Will do," Langdon said.

They both looked back towards the kitchen.

"Did you see her shoes?" Kelso said.

"Yep. For somebody who keeps her house as antiseptic as a hospital ER, it's odd to see her walking around with dirty shoes. I'll get some techs to sniff around the property."

"Good. Let's close things up with Ms. Dolenz for now, shall we?"

They returned to find Julia standing by the sink drinking a glass of water.

"Ms. Dolenz?" Kelso said. "Where do you keep your firearm?"

She turned around.

"*My* firearm?" She repeated.

"Yes. It's important that we see it."

"Very well. Let me show you..." She started walking away from the sink in his direction before Kelso held out his right arm like a traffic cop.

"Just tell me where to look, and I'll have officer Langdon retrieve it?"

She stopped, then she pointed over his shoulder in the direction of the living room.

"It's in the center drawer of the highboy. It's a 9mm."

"Where you were standing when your son threatened you?" Kelso said.

"Yes," she said.

182

Kelso looked over at Langdon and jerked his head towards the living room. Langdon left the kitchen and put on some vinyl gloves. He found the gun in the drawer and took it out to examine it. He smelled the weapon and there was no strong odor of gunpowder. He noticed that the safety was "off," and when he racked the slide, a bullet popped out of the chamber. In this state, all Julia Dolenz would have to do in order to get a shot off would be to pull the trigger. He picked the unspent bullet up off the floor and returned it as well as the gun to its drawer and returned to the kitchen.

"Ms. Dolenz's gun is where she said it would be," he reported to Kelso. Kelso nodded.

"We'll want to talk with you some more after this initial shock has subsided a bit if that's okay with you, Ms. Dolenz?"

She turned to look at them.

"Thanks awfully for your understanding," she said. "This has been an extraordinary day."

"One other thing," Kelso said. "Until we put complete closure to what's happened here today, I'll have to ask you not to travel far from Williamsburg? I know that you now have two funerals to plan and attend. Still..," His voice trailed off and he spread his hands.

"I understand." She said. "I don't wish that Richard's body go to the same funeral home as Reginald's. I don't know that I'll even put together a service for Richard. I'm afraid that I'm torn about that. I'll think about it and notify you when I've made a decision."

"That will be fine," Kelso said. "Is there anyone that I can contact for you?"

"That's very kind, Chief Kelso. But no. I'll call a dear friend and she'll spend the night with me, or rather, I'll spend the night with her."

"Sure," Kelso said. "Take care, Ms. Dolenz. We'll be in touch." He and Langdon left by way of the front door.

Julia walked back to the sink and looked out the window, and noted that a couple of young men wearing navy windbreakers that read 'POLICE" stenciled on their backs were poking around her back yard. They reached the potting shed, looked around a bit, and

183

then started heading back towards the house. She walked into the living room and to the bay window and looked out. Richard's remains, covered in a body bag, were being loaded inside an ambulance.

"Terry Grant... Good *God*, Richard," she said without emotion before she walked to her bedroom to change into different clothes for her visit to the funeral home.

Chapter 31

Jared McClure and Marty Tate arrived back in Williamsburg following what turned out to be a wild goose chase to Richmond. Together, they met with Chief Kelso and Officer Pete Langdon in their P.D. conference room where they reviewed their notes as well as photos taken at the residence, including pictures of the body of Richard Dolenz.

"It's like I told you guys on the phone," Kelso said. "Unlike what Julia Dolenz described to us, her son Richard was sitting in a chair with his gun when he had his seizure. Then, he fell off the chair leading with his left shoulder. Most of the armed offenders that I've run across over the years are standing up when they make their play, just like she told us that he was. So, this one's bugging me."

"It's enough to suspect foul play," McClure said. "She said that he confessed to killing her fiancé. That would be motive."

"Motive for revenge," said Marty Tate. "We told her that we suspected her son in Reginald White's murder when we interviewed her in the morning. How much do you want to bet that she invited her son to her house during the time that we were chasing our tails in Richmond?"

Silence ensued while all considered that. Finally, McClure spoke.

"So, where do you guys go from here?"

"Well, as you already know, unlike the TV police dramas, we can't get an autopsy report for another four to six weeks, given that we've requested special toxicology tests," Kelso said.

"We're thinking that she poisoned her son?" Tate said.

"Yep. The crime scene optics point in that direction." Kelso said.

"So, in the meantime, we'll ask Jared's State Police lab to run tests on the Browning that belonged to Richard Dolenz to see if it's a match for the murder weapon involved with the Reginald White and Kevin Berkley homicides. Then Jared can turn the weapon over to you, Marty, so that your team can compare it to the homicide and the attempted homicide cases that you have on the Outer Banks. That shouldn't take long."

"I'm good with that," Tate said.

"That sounds fine," McClure said.

"I've already petitioned a judge for a warrant to get the audio files - if they still exist - from Julia Dolenz's electronic personal assistant, Cordelia," Langdon said, before he went on to explain the 2015 Arkansas case.

"Interesting," McClure said. "I hope that produces something before a month is up."

"What did Julia Dolenz say about Richard's father having a heart attack in the U.K. years back?" Tate asked Langdon, who looked back at his notes.

"She told us that her late husband, George, had congenital heart disease and that perhaps this condition was passed on to Richard genetically." Langdon answered.

"Hmm…" McClure said. "There would have been an autopsy. Even an inquest. I've got some connections with Interpol. I'd be happy to dive a bit deeper into that story if that's okay with you, Ron?"

"Suits me," Kelso said. "He probably died in the mid nineteen nineties, would be my guess."

"Yeah," Tate said. "And a lot has changed with toxicology tests since then."

"So, if we find out that George Dolenz died of undetermined causes despite his heart condition, we might get even more suspicious about poisoning." McClure said.

"Exactly," Tate said, as he 'shot' at McClure with his right thumb and forefinger.

"Switching back to the deceased Richard Dolenz. The call that we had with Bill Etheridge, the FBI profiler…" McClure said to Tate.

"I remember. What about it?"

"He said that he wouldn't be surprised to find out that the guy that we were after had another identity."

"Yes, and we thought that was David Wiggins." Tate said.

"Exactly. He used that name with the women he was dating and the name that he listed on the dating website. But it turns out he had yet another identity. He was calling himself Terry Grant from a young age and claimed to have started killing kids when he was just a kid himself. Shit." McClure said.

"And that's why we couldn't find a BMW registered to a David Wiggins or a Richard Dolenz," Tate said.

McClure nodded.

"I'm going to have to follow up with the license bureau on how we screwed that one up. The photo on his driver's license should have been in the facial recognition system as Richard Dolenz," McClure said.

"Well, gentlemen," Kelso said. "That's all we've got at the moment. We'll stay in touch as things progress. Where are you going from here?"

"Back to Luray," McClure said. "Marty?"

"Back to Manteo," Tate said. "Let me know about the ballistics report and the status of the weapon as soon as you can?"

"Will do," Kelso said.

After a few more minutes, the men went their separate ways, connected to one another still with a case that wasn't closed. Julia Dolenz had told a tale that her son confessed to killing others when he was in junior high, boarding school, and college. Or was this a story made to cover up her own crime? Had she invited Richard to her house after she had gotten rid of McClure and Tate? Had she poisoned him? Had she turned herself into judge, jury, and executioner on an individual who admitted to killing her fiancé - even if that individual turned out to be her troubled only son?

Chapter 32

A week had passed. In that time, Virginia State police ballistics confirmed that the .22 caliber Browning Buckmaster pistol recovered from the body of Richard Dolenz was the weapon used to execute Reginald White as well as Kevin Berkley. The gun was couriered to the Dare County Sheriff's Office in Manteo, N.C. and positive confirmation was obtained to prove that the weapon had been used in the homicide of Dr. Phillip McCleney as well as the attempted homicide of Chip Walker. This left no doubt that the killer who Marty Tate and Jared McClure had been chasing was in fact, Richard Dolenz, a.k.a. David Wiggins, a.k.a. Terry Grant. Chief Ron Kelso made this notification to Julia Dolenz and Marty Tate made notifications to all those in the Outer Banks that were affected by the violence of the murderer, including Chip Walker and Kim Montgomery. He also congratulated his sketch artist who, as it turned out, played a key role in identifying the physical appearance of the mysterious offender.

Meanwhile, the remains of Reginald White were laid to rest in Cedar Grove Memorial Gardens on South Henry Street in Williamsburg. The visitation attracted many mourners, and Julia Dolenz was comforted to see that 'her Reggie' had positively affected so many lives. As per Reginald's last will and testament, the lion's share of his money and worldly possessions were left to his beloved Julia.

An autopsy on Richard Dolenz was conducted by a pathologist working out of the Norfolk Office of the Chief Medical Examiner. Organ as well as tissue samples were collected and stored in order to positively determine the exact cause of death. For the time being, the cause was noted as "Pending." At Julia Dolenz's request, his body was released by the coroner to a funeral home in Richmond where his remains were cremated and delivered by the funeral director to a cemetery on the east end of Richmond, a site and a city that Julia had no desire to visit.

Five days later, on a Monday morning, Chief Ron Kelso and Officer Pete Langdon were in his office reviewing larceny reports that had recently been called in, searching for a pattern to the crimes, when Brigid arrived at the door with a legal-sized envelope which had arrived by a courier service.

"Excuse me, gentlemen," Brigid said. "But this looks extremely important. I signed for it and it's addressed to you, Ron. It's from a company called Timespan. It's from their legal department." She held the envelope up and walked it over to Kelso, who pointed to Langdon. She handed him the envelope.

"Thanks, Brigid," Langdon said.

"Sure thing, Pete. I hope that it's good news?" She said and then she left the office.

Langdon sat staring at the envelope.

"Well?" Kelso said. "Aren't you going to open it?"

"Yeah. It's just that after two weeks' time, I'm thinking that this is going to be either a very politely stated 'Fuck You,' from their legal department, or its evidence that's going to put Julia Dolenz away for a long time."

Kelso made a *let's-get-on-with-it* rolling gesture with his right hand and Langdon opened the envelope.

"It's addressed to you, Ron." He said.

"It was your idea, so, you're gonna' read it - out loud - please."

Langdon nodded and began to read.

"Dear Chief Kelso, it is the customary policy of our company to vigorously protect our client's rights of privacy,'" he said out loud as he dropped the letter in his lap.

"See? It's a polite 'Fuck You,'" Langdon said.

"Keep reading!" Kelso said.

"Okay. It goes on with the typical legal smeagal blah blah blah about their privacy policy. Christ! These lawyers must get paid by the word count... Wait! Listen to this:

"That being duly noted, our legal department, upon reviewing the historical conversation between Julia Dolenz and her deceased son, and with the understanding that this conversation may be germane to your homicide investigation, we feel that it is our civic duty to share with you what remains of this conversation on our company's servers. Please use the following link on your computer to open the recorded conversation.' Then it gives us a link! This is fantastic!"

"What else does it say?"

189

"Ah… It goes on to say that 'conversations which are recorded by our Cordelia devices systematically delete portions of audio files as time passes in order to free up memory space. That being noted, our legal department believes that what remains of the historical conversation between J. and R. Dolenz can and should be used as evidence in the suspicious death of R. Dolenz.'

'Our customer may or may not be aware that they can retrieve or delete old recordings by opening the Timespan app on their smartphone, tap on the Settings menu, and then tap on History. There, they would find a large catalogue of recordings. They could select the recording that they'd like to review, and tap the Play icon to listen to it.'"

"I wonder if she knows." Kelso said.

"It may not matter. Let me get to my computer and I'll plug in the link that they sent us."

"Be my guest," Kelso said.

Pete Langdon went back to his computer in the squad room, loaded the link, and pressed 'Play.'

After listening to what was on the recorder, he felt his face go flush. He picked up his phone and called the Office of the Chief Medical Examiner and found the pathologist that was working on the Richard Dolenz case. After giving her the background, he gave her what he had found on the Cordelia recording.

"It's aconite that you're looking for," he said.

"That should be straightforward enough to test, now that we know what we're looking for," she said. "Good work, Detective Langdon."

"Thanks, but, it's Officer Langdon. Pete Langdon."

"Okay. But go tell that boss of yours that it should be Detective. I'll call you when we get the official results."

"Thanks, and I'm off to see the boss now. Have a good day, Doctor.

Langdon returned to Ron Kelso's office and stuck his head in the door. Kelso looked up from his desk.

"Well? Is it any good?" Kelso asked.

"It's good enough for homicide in the first degree. And I phoned the medical examiner's office. They're going to be testing for the presence of aconite."

"That's what you learned from recording? Great work, Pete!"

190

"Thanks. I can't wait to watch her face when we play back the recording."

"We'll have that opportunity, soon, I'm sure. In the meantime, let's get started on getting a hold of a judge and draw up an arrest and search warrant for the person and property of Ms. Julia Dolenz. I'd also like to get a bloodhound in her backyard. Give our K9 guy a heads up."

"Will do," Langdon said.

"Exceptional work, Pete. Well done." Kelso said.

"Let's just hope that a sharp defense attorney doesn't get her off the hook in court."

"That's not our job to worry about, it's the D.A.'s., as you know. Call Jared McClure and give him what we've got. He said he has connections with Interpol. Maybe he can track down the police who were involved in the investigation of George Dolenz's death over in the U.K... If he hasn't already, that is. I'm certain that they'd find all of this quite compelling. After all, there's no statute of limitations if his death is now reopened as a homicide."

"Good idea," Langdon said before he left the office in search of a magistrate and his phone.

Chapter 33

It was early September in Williamsburg. The sun's rays glinted in the early morning upon the spires of Bruton Parish Church as well as the Wren Building, the oldest academic building in use in America, at the entranceway to The College of William and Mary. In the historic area, Leicester Longwool sheep and their young offspring were eating blades of grass covered in morning dew in a pasture at the intersection of Nassau and Francis streets. So were the oxen and horses, awake and enjoying the sunshine of a new day before the tourists would fill the cobblestone streets and marvel at the authenticity of the Historic Area.

Back at the street Julia Dolenz called home, the final elements of the police dragnet had been formed and were converging on her house from different geographic directions. From the northeast a Virginia State Police cruiser carried Lt. Jared McClure and Commander Graham Shaw of New Scotland Yard, fresh from a flight from London's Heathrow Airport. From the southeast, Sheriff Marty Tate was driving up to the peninsula from Manteo. A K9 unit from Williamsburg P.D. was heading down the quiet streets with a Bloodhound aboard. Bloodhounds have been known to successfully track scent trails that were over one hundred hours old and over fifty miles long. Finally, a Williamsburg Police cruiser carrying Ron Kelso and Pete Langdon arrived.

The five law enforcement officers as well as the K9 unit parked and dismounted their vehicles and had a short conference on the sidewalk in front of the house. It was decided that Kelso and Langdon would knock on the door and present Ms. Dolenz with the search warrant that covered the contents of her home, personal electronic equipment, and authority for the K9 to search the grounds. Once she was served with the search warrant, the K9 officer would be deployed to the backyard, and the other three law enforcement officers would enter the home and Julia Dolenz would be served with a warrant for her arrest for murder in the first degree.

Julia opened the front door. She was dressed in business casual chic this morning in colors of brown and cream, and she said that she was on her way to a breakfast with her book club members at the Williamsburg Inn. She didn't look like a woman who recently lost a fiancé AND a child. After she was served with the search warrant, she objected strongly to the presence of the police force outside her home as well as to the warrant.

As the K9 unit made their way to the backyard, Tate, McClure, and Shaw made their way up the sidewalk and also entered the home. At McClure's suggestion, the identity of Shaw was kept obtuse for the moment. He was simply introduced as Detective Shaw.

Julia took in this Detective Shaw standing in her living room. Tall and lanky, with salt and pepper hair and a brown mustache, he was wearing a Harris Tweed sport coat over thin whale corduroy slacks and brown penny loafers. There was a tincture of discomforting familiarity about him that gave her a turn, but she had more pressing things she needed to know about the reasons for such a large police presence in her home.

It was decided that Kelso should take the lead since it was his homicide and jurisdiction. Marty Tate had been invited out of courtesy so that he could assist in putting closure to the Dolenz matter.

"Won't all of you please sit down?" Julia Dolenz said. "I hope that this won't take too long as my friends at the book club are waiting for me."

With the exception of Chief Kelso, they took seats on chairs and a couch in different parts of the living room. She was standing in front of the cherry wood highboy when Kelso put his hand on her shoulder and directed her to step aside. She complied, and he moved forward and opened the center drawer and removed her Glock 19 handgun and handed it over to Langdon.

"I say," Julia said. "Once again I say, what's this all about?"

"Please take a seat, Ms. Dolenz. We have some ground to cover with you this morning," Kelso said. She took a seat near the by window in the very chair that Richard had been sitting in weeks ago when he died of aconite poisoning. Kelso stayed standing.

"First, ballistics confirmed that the gun that your son had in his possession last month was the weapon used in the homicides of Mr. Kevin Berkley of Virginia, Dr. Phillip McCleney of the Outer Banks of North Carolina, as well as in the attack on the person of Mr. Chip Walker, also of the Outer Banks. Finally, and most regrettably, the weapon was used to kill Mr. Reginald White of Williamsburg, Virginia."

She took in the news in calm fashion. She pursed her lips and exhaled an audible breath of air.

"As I told you, Richard was mad. He was calling himself Terry Grant. He went 'round the bend. I'm sickened of course, that I seemed to have raised a serial killer who took my own Reggie from me," she said as she took a handkerchief out of her blazer and wiped her eye.

"Yes, he was no doubt a violent young man," Kelso said. "But, here's the thing… Our Medical Examiner and pathologist both agreed that he was in fine physical shape and had a strong heart. He didn't inherit a genetic heart condition from his father."

"How on earth would you conclude that?" she said with a tone of annoyance.

Kelso nodded over to Langdon, who opened up his field briefcase, placed her weapon inside it and withdrew a manila file.

"It's all here in the official autopsy report," Langdon said.

She looked at him but didn't move.

There was a loud knock by the door of the kitchen. Tate got up and went into the kitchen to answer it.

"Forgive me, all. I'll be back in a moment," he said.

"Such clever men you all are. *And,* you're all with the *police,*" she said. "I've seen stories like this on your American TV police dramas. You're trying to get at something that you think that I have and that you're missing in the case of Richard's death. 'Oh, what a tangled web we weave, when first we practice to deceive!'"

"Shakespeare?" Langdon said.

"Negative," Tate said as he entered the space carrying a large plastic bag with a dirty pillowcase placed inside it. "That would be Sir Walter Scott, and you won't believe what we have, Ms. Dolenz."

"Whatever it is that you're carrying there, Sheriff, isn't mine. I've never seen it before. What? Did some young neighborhood hoodlums come running about and put something in my backyard? I saw that policeman and the bloodhound out back. How dare you dig up my yard."

"The search warrant covers it, ma'am," Kelso said.

"I'm afraid that things are much worse than you think, Ms. Dolenz," Kelso said.

194

"We have a warrant for your arrest."

"Arrest!? Christ! For what bloody crime are you charging me with?!" she demanded.

"Homicide," Shaw finally spoke as he stood up and drew closer to her chair. "Homicide in the first degree."

His British accent sent chills down her spine. She was beginning to recognize this tall, quiet man.

"Who exactly are you, *Detective* Shaw?" she asked.

"In fact, I would be Commander Graham Shaw of New Scotland Yard. I was a young Inspector twenty-two years ago when I worked the case of your husband George's mysterious death. No doubt, it would be difficult to recognize me today. Still, I came here as a result of a courtesy call made by the Virginia State Police," Shaw explained as he jerked his head in the direction of Jared McClure.

"What does George's case have to do with any of this business?" she said. She was stalling. She was feeling the net draw closed. She was afraid of what to ask next, but, she had to know. "What does the autopsy report show?" she asked Pete Langdon.

"That your son Richard was poisoned by a substance called aconite." he said.

"Rubbish! I've never heard of such a thing," she said as she waived her right arm dismissively in the air.

"I'll need you to stand up Ms. Dolenz," Kelso said.

Langdon walked over to her and cuffed her and Mirandized her. "You have the right to remain silent," he said. "Anything you say can and will be used against you in a court of law."

"Oh shut up!" She said as she cut him off. "I've seen enough police T.V. shows to know what you're going to say next."

"You have the right to talk to a lawyer and have him present while you are being questioned." Langdon ignored her protest and finished the Miranda warning.

"Please take a seat," Langdon said as he finished. She complied.

Langdon returned to where he had been previously seated and took out his iPad. He put his finger on it and held it out with the volume turned up high.

As dread began to fill up her brain she heard the complete conversation from one month ago between herself and her doomed son. He finished playing the final part of the recording:

I executed your father for his crime of lust, and now I'm going to execute you for murdering my Reggie and for all the others you've maimed...

You see, I whipped up this little batch of aconite yesterday. You do know that I grow monkshood in my flower garden out back, don't you, Terry?

You wouldn't kill... your own son, Richard is heard to gasp.

No. I won't have to. The aconite will though. Your iced tea. Remember, Terry?"

"Where on *earth* did *that* rubbish come from?" Julia said.

"From Cordelia. Your electronic personal assistant," Langdon said matter-of-factly.

He put his iPad in his briefcase and stood up and nodded to Kelso.

"We have the audio recording. We have the autopsy report. We have probably found the glass and the residual poison that you used on your son inside that bag that Sheriff Tate is holding. We also have the crime scene photos that prove that Richard was sitting down when he allegedly threatened you." Kelso said.

"Fuck you up your arse!" She screamed at Kelso. "He *did* threaten me! It's probably there on a section of that tape that you didn't play back. Richard was a dangerous killer! You said so yourself!"

"When you saw your son at the door last month, already sensing that he had killed Reginald White, you let him in. You probably doctored up the poison perhaps the previous day. Our officers noted that they found monkshood growing in your garden last month. That's a good source of aconite. You could have left Richard locked out on the front porch that morning and called 911. But, we feel that you had invited him here perhaps on the pretense of talking about restoring his allowance."

Julia shot McClure and Tate a hateful gaze.

"So you shouldn't have taken it upon yourself to play judge, jury, and executioner," Tate said.

He turned over the plastic bag to Langdon.

"You knew that Lt. McClure and I were on our way to apprehend your son."

"But he came here *instead*. To *kill* me, I say!" Julia deflected to her deceased son.

"Your son had two times the lethal amount of aconite in his system, according to the Medical Examiner," Kelso said. "You knew that he'd be dead within 30 - 45 minutes of drinking the iced tea that you served him."

She rocked in her chair.

"With the fortune that Reggie left me, I'll get the best legal counsel in the country to defend me," she said, looking at Kelso.

Commander Shaw spoke next.

"You have every right to do so, of course, Ms. Dolenz. But you should also take into account that if that very clever attorney manages to keep you out of the American penal system, we'll have a cell waiting for you back in England where you'll stand charged with the premeditated murder of your husband, George. My superiors are now very keen to re-open the case and to have your husband's remains exhumed, should it come to that. Toxicology tests are much more sophisticated today than they were in the 1990's. Still, I think that these Yanks might find you some sort of country club prison where you'll be placed for a long time."

"Piss off!" She said.

"Let's go," Kelso said to Langdon.

As she was being led out her front door by Pete Langdon, Marty Tate got her attention.

"Ms. Dolenz?" he shouted out.

Langdon paused and she looked back at Tate with scorn. She said nothing.

"Galatians 6:8," he said.

She pursed her lips and shook her head.

"*Stuff* it, Sheriff," she said as she looked in front of her and was led out the door. He smirked and waved as she was led away.

Commander Shaw came round and shook Marty Tate's hand.

"I must confess that I'm not up to snuff when it comes to St. Paul's Epistles," he said. "Tell me how that one goes? She seemed to recognize its meaning immediately."

Tate repeated the quote from memory.

"Quite right. And very appropriate," Shaw said. "Are you a religious man, Sheriff Tate?"

"No, Commander. Just a spiritual one."

Jared McClure approached the two men.

"Well. It's been great working with you guys," McClure said as all of them shook hands.

"Likewise," Marty Tate said.

"All of you have made an extraordinary team, I must say," Graham Shaw said.

"This has been such nasty business. I must say that when you called me, Jared, and gave me the particulars about your suspicions about Julia Dolenz, it didn't altogether surprise me."

"Oh?" McClure said.

"That verbal display that all of you saw in here a moment ago? That's what we at Scotland Yard saw from her twenty years ago. Completely defiant. We couldn't break her because we didn't have the proof and she knew it. But today, she had to face the truth and the evidence. Brilliant. Well done, all of you." Shaw said.

"What was brilliant was Pete Langdon figuring out how to retrieve a recorded conversation from her personal assistant," Tate said.

"Boy, I'll say," McClure said. "That was an out of the park home run."

"True," Shaw said.

"However, I think that the optics of the physical crime scene told a lot about what had happened here, and eventually, the medical examiner would have found the traces of aconite," McClure said.

"Richard Dolenz really screwed the pooch when he went after Reginald White," Tate said.

"Yep," McClure said. "If he had left him well enough alone, he might still be alive."

"Yeah. And don't forget, thanks to Kim Montgomery, we would have made a run for him anyway. It's too bad that we didn't get the chance to interrogate him in order to find out why he killed those men," Tate said. "At least have the chance to see if his story tallied with what Bill Etheridge told us."

Graham Shaw looked confused.

"Special Agent Etheridge from the FBI's Behavioral Analysis Unit," McClure said to him.

"Ah. One of those profiler blokes?" Shaw said.

"Exactly, Tate said. "He told us that his theory was that the person who turned out to be Richard was actually raging against a strong female authority figure."

"His mother Julia… my word," Shaw said.

"So his motive in killing Reginald White may have been more than just money," Tate said.

"He *really* wanted to hurt his mother very badly," McClure said.

"Yep. But it turned out that he totally underestimated who he was fucking with," Tate said.

"Yep. He had absolutely no idea," McClure said.

"It turned out that Julia was a Janus figure just like her son." Tate said.

"Two faces." Shaw said. "One good, the other, evil."

Tate nodded.

"Well, I have to catch a flight back to London," Shaw said.

"Yes, and I will be happy to drive you there. Gentlemen?" McClure said.

The men shook hands, got into their vehicles, and went their respective ways, and Julia Dolenz was back at the Williamsburg police department being booked for murder one.

Epilogue

It was Saturday on the first weekend of October in Duck, North Carolina. Mr. & Mrs. Chip Walker were celebrating at their wedding reception being held at the sound side of the Sanderling Resort. Earlier in the day, the wedding ceremony was officiated ocean side within view of the resort's main inn. The late afternoon reception had been chosen by Chip and Kim with the hopes that the weather would be fair. In fact, it was a beautiful early autumn day. So the wedding guests would be treated to another fantastic Outer Banks sunset along the banks of the Currituck Sound.

A large white tent had been erected, and inside, enough round tables and chairs to accommodate the seventy-five or so invited guests. Soft jazz provided by a local trio filled the air. Atop the tables were glass vases filled with a sunset gladiolus mix of peach, pink, purple and white long stemmed flowers.

At the head table, the groom wore a dark gray traditional cutaway morning coat tuxedo. The bride proudly wore the dress that was worn by her mother, and her head was adorned with a brand new white Victorian riding hat. Also seated at the head table flanking the newlyweds to their left and right was the wedding party.

At a round table near the front were seated Paul and Megan Treadwell, Mary Kay and Geoffrey Cullipher, and Marty and Elizabeth Tate. All of the guests raved about the delectable food that had been expertly prepared and catered by Frederick Douglas Books and a pair of his sous chefs from the Brown Pelican restaurant. When the celebratory meal was concluded, Chip and Kim Walker made their rounds to each of the tables in order to greet and thank their guests.

"They make for a fine-looking couple, don't they?" Megan said.

"They do, indeed," Mrs. C. said and her husband nodded in agreement.

"They say that about every couple at every wedding," Paul said as he took a pull on his glass of champagne.

"Oh, stop being so non-romantic, husband," Megan said as she nudged Paul.

"Martin can be romantic," Elizabeth said - or Lizbeth as she preferred to be called by her friends. Lizbeth was tall and graceful with shoulder-length auburn hair and striking, deep blue eyes."

"He *can*?" Paul said incredulously.

Marty flipped the middle finger of his left hand back at Paul so that Lizbeth couldn't see the crude gesture. Paul smiled back at him.

"Uh huh," Lizbeth said. "In fact, I know that he hasn't forgotten that we have a special wedding anniversary coming up soon."

She looked over at her husband who was dressed formally with a suit and tie for the special occasion. It was a rarity to see Tate outside of his service uniform.

"Roger that," he said back to his wife as he gave her a wink.

"It will be twenty-five years married on the fifteenth of this month," he said so that all could hear.

Everyone around the table gave them a respectful and hearty round of applause and a chorus of 'congratulations.'

"Hey, Marty," Paul said.

"Oh, this ought to be good," Tate sarcastically whispered to his wife.

"You know that I take sadistic pleasure in putting you on the spot."

"Uh-huh," Tate said, as he rolled his left hand in a *please-get-on-with-this* gesture, before he took a sip from his longneck bottle of Carolina Blonde beer.

"So, twenty-five years married calls for a special gift. You'd better make it a good one this year."

"I'll drink to that," Lizbeth said a she reached for her glass of mimosa to toast Paul.

"A couple of days away from that stressful job that he has would be the greatest gift for me," she said. "You know, we haven't had a proper travelling vacation in five years."

"After twenty-five years I would've thought that you'd enjoy me being away from the house," Marty said.

"Not on our wedding anniversary, silly. Especially this one," Lizbeth said.

Marty sat quietly as the others around the table engaged in conversation. Marty frowned and he pursed his lips. He took a deep breath as he leaned back in his chair, and with his right hand, he reached into his jacket's left lapel pocket, and took out a white, letter-sized envelope.

"I was going to present this to you later, dear," he explained as he handed the envelope to Lizbeth.

"But, I can't resist shutting up my smart-assed friend over there," Tate said as he jerked his head in Paul's direction.

Tate nodded at Treadwell with a big grin on his face. Paul chuckled.

"Go ahead and open it," Tate said.

"I most certainly will," Lizbeth said. "But is this for my eyes only or can I share whatever's inside with our friends?"

"That's *your* call," Marty said as he took another small swig of beer.

She opened the envelope and noted the travel agency masthead on a single piece of stationary that she began to unfold completely. After she read the contents, she put the paper down and she leaned over and took her husband's face in her hands and gave him an extended smooch on his lips.

"What is it, Lizbeth?" Mrs. C. said as she looked over at her.

Everyone around the table knew that she'd be the first one to make an inquiry, since Mary Kay held the unofficial title of the Town of Duck Gossip.

Lizbeth took the piece of paper in her hands again and spoke with joy evident in her voice.

"It's a travel itinerary, everyone! A wonderful, thoughtful, itinerary if I've ever seen one. We're flying out of Richmond on the 15th, and we'll be spending two nights at the Harraseeket Inn in Freeport, Maine. Marty knows how much I love Maine, and how I love to go shopping at L.L. Bean."

"That's fantastic!" Megan shouted. "Good going, Marty!"

"Well, selfishly, I get to enjoy all the lobster rolls that I care to eat, and drink craft beers made in Maine," Marty said.

"Wait everybody," Lizbeth said. "There's more."

"Do tell," Mrs. C. said.

"Next, we're driving north to one of my favorite places on earth. We're going to spend three whole nights at the Bar Harbor Inn!"

"Hey, that's where Chip and Kim are heading for their honeymoon," Megan said.

"Isn't that where your daughter Mary attends college?" Paul said.

"Yep," Marty said. "We write the checks out to the College of the Atlantic, located right in Bar Harbor. We can see Mary."

"We should take a day and go to Acadia National Park with her," Lizbeth said.

"That's kinda' what I had in mind," Marty said. Lizbeth leaned over and whispered into her husband's ear.

"I love you, Martin. Thank you so much," she said as she gave his hand a squeeze. He nodded and smiled back at her.

Another round of applause from the friends around the table.

"That's a nice gift, Martin," Paul said with a note of mocking in his voice.

"Bite me, Treadwell," he said as he pointed at his friend.

"Excuse me, everyone!" Chef Books belted out to the crowd.

"For all those that are interested, especially those of you from out of town, the sun is setting over the sound and it sure is a pretty sight to see."

About half of the crowd got up from their chairs and headed for the tent's west openings. Marty stood up and helped Lizbeth out of her chair like a proper gentleman.

"We're going for a walk by the ocean," he said. "We'll be back later."

"Okay. Have fun you two," Megan said as she waved at them.

After crossing Duck Road, Marty and Lizbeth cut through the Resort's grounds. They reached the wooden walkway that led to the beach and removed their footwear, and Marty took off his tie and rolled up his pant legs. Once on the beach they were walking north, hand in hand. In their direction, the Currituck Beach lighthouse tower in Corolla began to flash its first order Fresnel lens, which can be seen for 18 nautical miles.

Ghost crabs scuttled along with the rhythm of the waves that lapped the shore. Marty took out a small Maglite so that they could 'shine' the ghost crabs while the tiny critters scavenged for carrion.

As the night grew darker, the Atlantic took on a luminescence of glowing green. This fascinating phenomena in the waves is the product of millions of marine microbes known as phytoplankton, swimming together and generating this rare optical display.

"Let's stop here a moment, dear?" Lizbeth said as she pointed north to the blinking light from the Currituck lighthouse.

"Do you remember the cadence?" Marty said.

"Three seconds on, off for 17 seconds," she said.

"Let's count and see if that's still right?" Marty said.

And they did so, and the historic light flashed out its beam in the very cadence that Lizbeth had described. Stars appeared overhead. The gulls and the osprey were done. Another winter would arrive, together with strong tidal storms that would once again threaten the shorelines of towns south of here such as Waves and Buxton and Salvo. And when the storms cleared away, those Outer Bankers who were granted permission to rebuild would go back to work repairing their homes and businesses in hopes of enjoying another summer in the sun.

Then, another tourist season would begin, and Sheriff Marty Tate would still be on the job.

ACKNOWLEDGEMENTS

The author gratefully acknowledges the invaluable help of Evelyn Schaeffer with the editing of this book. She made this a better story. Thanks also to the many family members and friends in Ohio and in Rogers City, Michigan who supported me and encouraged me throughout this project. You know who you are. Cheers to all.

A most loving thank you goes out to Charlene for her patience, guidance and invaluable feedback as always!

A special helping of cat nip goes out to our seventeen year old cat, Smokey, and our eleven year old cat, Baxter, who watched over me - or napped beside me - while I clacked away on my keyboard. Sadly, they left us within three days of one another this past February. They are sorely missed and will never be forgotten. They would be happy to know that our eight year old cat, Homer, now has a new companion named Buster who is keeping him company.

All of the ways that technology can help us or harm us as described in this body of work, are true. Social media and some of the newest devices on our planet opens us up to new worlds, where unfortunately, clever people with ill - intentions can do us harm if we fail to be vigilant in protecting our data and our identities.

Finally, thanks for the inspiration: Thomas Tryon, John Cash, Edgar Allen Poe, Sir Arthur Conan Doyle, P.D. James, Ruth Rendell, Rita Mae Brown, Michael Connelly, and most especially, Robert B. Parker.

And to the people and places of the Outer Banks of North Carolina.

Colin Beckett

July, 2018

Praise for Colin Beckett's Debut Thriller

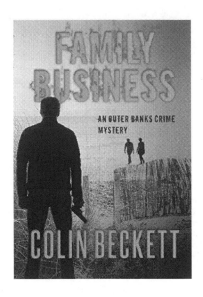

Editorial Reviews

"A grim, thrilling mystery. From this book's cold-blooded opening, readers know that they're in for a story told by a master of suspense. The patient, calculating and terrifying style that Colin Beckett puts on display in Family Business is unique and chilling, making it nearly impossible to put it down. Like all great thrillers, the novel provides readers with virtuous heroes to root for, a suspect to fear and loathe, and all the action in between to satisfy a morbid fascination with human nature's darker side." *John Staughton, Self-Publishing Review,* **Five Star Review**

"The point of view of the murderer, too, is effective; he's terrifyingly scrupulous...it's the largely unknown killer who makes the grandest impression." *- Kirkus Reviews*

22839044R00115

Made in the USA
Columbia, SC
03 August 2018